But Not Too Bold

By **HACHE PUEYO**

But Not Too Bold

AS H. PUEYO

A Study in Ugliness & outras histórias

HACHE PUEYO

But Not Too Bold

TOR PUBLISHING GROUP · NEW YORK

This is a work of fiction. All of the characters, organizations, and events portrayed in this novella are either products of the author's imagination or are used fictitiously.

BUT NOT TOO BOLD

Copyright © 2025 by Hache Pueyo

All rights reserved.

A Tordotcom Book
Published by Tom Doherty Associates / Tor Publishing Group
120 Broadway
New York, NY 10271

www.torpublishinggroup.com

Tor® is a registered trademark of Macmillan Publishing Group, LLC.

Library of Congress Cataloging-in-Publication Data

Names: Pueyo, H., author.
Title: But not too bold / Hache Pueyo.
Other titles: Bem mal me quer. English
Description: First edition. | New York : Tor Publishing Group, 2025.
Identifiers: LCCN 2024038871 | ISBN 9781250376633 (hardcover) | ISBN 9781250910530 (ebook)
Subjects: LCGFT: Monster fiction. | Horror fiction. | Novels.
Classification: LCC PQ9698.426.U43 B4613 2025 | DDC 869.3/5—dc23/eng/20240826
LC record available at https://lccn.loc.gov/2024038871

Our books may be purchased in bulk for promotional, educational, or business use. Please contact your local bookseller or the Macmillan Corporate and Premium Sales Department at 1-800-221-7945, extension 5442, or by email at MacmillanSpecialMarkets@macmillan.com.

First Edition: 2025

Printed in the United States of America

0 9 8 7 6 5 4 3 2 1

But Not Too Bold

The old keeper of the keys was dead, but no one heard her muffled scream, her crushed bones, or the iron keys that fell on the floor, clinking and clanking. In fact, they only knew she was gone when a note arrived to the second floor, delivered by the empty elevator:

HIRE A NEW KEEPER OF THE KEYS; URGENT; BEFORE DAWN.

The maid that found the typewritten letter—the owner of the house could not handle a pen, but her long fingers moved comfortably on typewriter keys—nearly fainted. Asking for a new employee was as good as a death certificate. Everyone knew that.

It was then that they had to call Dália at ten in the morning, after removing all the belongings of the deceased from the house. When she unlocked Ms. Matilde's bedroom, Dália expected to find the former keeper of the keys, but there were only empty wardrobes and a bed whose covers and pillows had been plucked until only the bare mattress remained. Even the colorful beads that Matilde hung from the headboard had been scoured from the room, like she had never existed in the first place.

Only two familiar faces remained: a tarantula in a tank and the majordomo, a brooding man known as Lionel.

"I did not expect to promote you under such circumstances," started Lionel, looking defeated with his elbows on his thighs, a ghost sitting on the velvet armchair. Lionel had not shaved from one day to the other, and his brown hair fell on his face like a curtain clawed by a cat. "But she didn't give us a choice. Time to go to the third floor, Dália."

Had she been any other employee, those words would have felt like a slap, but she was Dália, only Dália, who had been trained her entire life to assume this role. *Swallow your fear,* she had learned with Matilde. *You must learn to avoid being seen.* At the age of eight, when Matilde took her to the third floor for the first time, her mentor instructed her to cover her nose with a perfumed handkerchief as she walked on the carpet smelling like carrion, and smiled proudly when Dália did not throw up.

"What happened?"

"What do you think?" Lionel left the embellished envelope on the bed and stood up. His spider, a cobalt blue tarantula, observed Dália from her owner's pointy shoulder. "She was devoured, like everyone else. It's true that she rarely eats her keepers, but . . . It doesn't matter. What matters is that Anatema requires a replacement right away."

Dália looked at the tank. The Brazilian black was still immobile in her cage, partially covered by leaves. She imagined her next to her own pet tarantula, a Chilean rose: one tank over the other, or side by side, under the window.

"When do I start?"

The preparations took a good deal of the day. It was not

uncommon, not in the Capricious House, to have all the employees rearranging schedules and rooms after someone's death, but usually, it was one of the brides and, sometimes, one of the maids who worked on the third floor.

The eccentric house had been commissioned by Anatema herself; she even brought the renowned architect Arnau Torroella i Fajó, one of the most important names of Catalan Modernisme with Gaudí, Montaner, and Cadafalch, to realize a most ambitious construction. A neo-Gothic palazzo with Germanic inspiration, a flat facade with graffito, crowned by a stepped Flemish pediment adorned by ornate tiles and macabre creatures, gargoyle-like.

The interior had three floors and an ample attic, all of them as richly decorated as the exterior. Stained glass in every window; a music room covered in tapestries; two enormous kitchens with tiled floors; a fireplace of sculpted stone so large that an entire troop could march out of it; colorful chandeliers, cabinets, wallpapers; and comfortable bedrooms for every single employee of the house.

The intention was clear: the house had to reflect its mistress.

The Capricious House, or Casa Caprichosa, as Torroella i Fajó named it, became a regional landmark, partially hidden by the large field of poppies that surrounded it. It was near many villages, and everyone knew that the person who lived there was as wealthy as she was solitary, but they were partially wrong in their assessments.

The owner was not a person. And she was not solitary—she was hiding.

By the end of the afternoon, Dália was ready and standing in front of the elevator on the second floor. The elevator was another peculiar construction, with a gate made of copper and wrought iron, a secondary folding door made of varnished mahogany, a half-length mirror, a Persian rug on the floor, and levers under the buttons. Nothing was allowed to be ordinary in the Capricious House.

Dália crossed the double doors.

"Remember," warned Lionel, even though she already knew what he would say. "Never mispronounce her name. Ah-nah-teh-mah, and you must say it very clearly, not Ana*the*ma. Don't look at her face. Don't contradict her. Don't . . ."

"Lionel," Dália interrupted. "I'm ready."

The man was as white as a sheet of paper. He took an indigo ribbon from his pocket, one she recognized as Matilde's, and gave it to her.

"For your hair," said Lionel. The two of them wore the same standard suit that every other employee of the upper floors wore. The difference was that his uniform had a turquoise cravat, representing the second story, while the indigo of the ribbon represented the third. After he spoke, Lionel gave her a compact bottle, which Dália left in the pocket of her jacket. "Anatema's favorite."

After the doors closed, the elevator began to ascend slowly, and Dália turned to look at the mirror. She untied her old turquoise ribbon and wrapped the new one around her curls, arranging them on the back of her neck with a simple bow. Two strands fell on her face, as black as her eyes and the rest of her clothes.

Outside, the spiral staircase coiled around the elevator glass panes, revealing the mint-colored walls of the third floor, with its golden peacocks and blooming branches.

With a jolt, the elevator stopped, and the iron gate opened with a clunk. The corridor carpet had a saying embroidered on it:

BE BOLD, BE BOLD

The highest floor—save for the attic, accessed only by Anatema and her brides—was even more ostentatious than those below. It had the same Art Nouveau decoration as the rest of the house, but with gilded handrails, crystal china cabinets, endless shelves filled with books, and, of course, tarantulas.

Dália crouched to take one of the spiders in her hands, leaving her on the stairs. Beyond its immoderate architecture, the Capricious House had two peculiarities: the poppies of all colors that kept growing even after being harvested, and the tarantulas that appeared everywhere. It was all so excessive that it became an issue, and the employees had to be creative to deal with the circumstances.

With the poppies, they brewed teas, arranged flowers, envisioned gastronomic decorations, and prepared morphine for the sick; they also smoked opium, sold paregoric elixirs, and produced laudanum. The latter was consumed by the owner in colossal amounts. To deal with the tarantula plague, they cooked the spiders or kept them as pets. They had the dalmatians for hunting, the chickens and goats for eggs and milk, and the spiders in tanks, their loyal companions day after day.

Dália walked slowly. She knew the third floor like the palm of her hand. Matilde taught her every corner and crevice before she could even dream of going upstairs, just like she taught her what each key was for and how to distinguish one from another. She could see them when she closed her eyes: a brass mortise key, slightly crooked, three Yale keys, almost identical except for discreet lines on their thin sides, a key made of pure gold . . .

Dália stopped in front of the closed door of the library,

where the phrase she found in front of the elevator continued in front of every room:

BE BOLD, BUT NOT TOO BOLD

She knocked.

KEEPER OF THE KEYS?

Dália winced at the sound. The voice was at the same time a whisper and a booming echo, and the entire corridor shuddered with her.

"Madam?"

The double doors swung open.

At first glance, there was no one inside. The library was in complete disarray: disorganized papers were scattered across the desk, and the heavy wooden doors had crumpled part of the thick, red rug. The shelves had ancient and recent tomes in varying states of repair, some of them coverless and coming apart at the seams. A brown tarantula walked between her legs and fled to the corridor.

Dália looked up.

The owner of the house observed her from a cove in the ceiling, and there was no other word to describe her except gigantic. In fact, she was so big that, if she stretched all eight articulated limbs, the space of the library would not be sufficient for her, and Dália doubted the corridor would be, either. Her legs folded like a spider's, ending in three funneled fingers, thirty centimeters each, and her thin body reminded Dália—if only in outline—of a horribly narrow and tall woman. Though in reality, she suspected that the body was divided into two arachnid tagmata.

Anatema blinked from her lower lid upward; even the slightest, most commonplace action was unnatural when she did it. The movement brought Dália's attention to

Anatema's face, the only part of her that was vaguely human. An oval shape, a nose plastered on the skull, two eyes of the deepest ink blue, a nictitating membrane, and lips with lines like a ventriloquist's dummy.

Lips which, Dália knew, unfolded like the lie they were to reveal the true mouth underneath, starting from the nostrils and continuing down to the end of the esophagus, displaying powerful chelicerae where her jaw should have been, and several rows of sharp fangs that went from her gums to her throat.

Anatema blinked again, and her neck, thicker than Dália's entire body, extended until her face was in front of Dália's. Nose to nose, she asked:

WHAT IS YOUR NAME, NEW KEEPER OF THE KEYS?

Dália almost tumbled down to the rug. Anatema's voice was an animal's screech, barely comprehensible, and fury dripped from it like saliva from a tongue. Close up, Dália could see that her human face was a mask, nothing but the aggressive mimicry of an arthropod searching for prey.

She lowered her eyes. "Dália, madam."

Anatema curved her neck, considering. Her face was still, but the lines that hid her mouth moved almost imperceptibly.

DO YOU KNOW WHY YOU ARE HERE?

"Ms. Matilde passed away, and you requested my services."

Dália understood, under such a close inspection, why the brides that came from time to time always fled after finally seeing their suitor. It was a terrible sight indeed, but a hypnotic one as well. Her silvery skin, bedecked with minuscule scales, glimmered even in the half-light produced by the curtains, and it acquired shades of blue as it continued down her trachea. The velvet robe, indigo colored and tied carelessly around her waist, covered her four upper limbs and her torso, and her long hair, also part of the mimicry, was straight, black, and gray.

Anatema widened her mouth. The skin unglued from her face like the petals of a flower, revealing complex sequences of fangs, teeth, pincers, and a turquoise tongue so long that she wrapped it around Dália's neck to bring her closer.

"The old keeper of the keys was a thief." Her voice now came directly from her windpipe. Dália did not dare to move. Anatema took the flask of laudanum that Lionel had given Dália from the pocket of her jacket and hid it inside her own robes. "Are you one, too?"

"I swear I am not." Dália was immobile, a statue like so many others in the house. She was not afraid. All the employees knew they could die for any given mishap, but they also knew how to calm their mistress down. "What did Ms. Matilde steal from you?"

Anatema used one of her back legs to reach the heavy bunch of keys from the desk. She dropped it into Dália's hands, who noticed one she had never seen before: a tiny little key, made of copper, stained with still-red blood.

"Come to the treasury and you will see."

What Anatema called a treasury was the tall wall in front of the elevator, with hundreds of little marquetry doors, drawer over drawer like an endless cabinet. T H E K E Y, said Anatema, unlocking the rolling ladder as her voice reverberated inside Dália, who climbed the steps toward the door with inlaid marble she was pointing at.

The redness on the key would not go away, no matter how many times she tried to remove the blood with her nail—and it was the one she had to use to unlock the little door so the drawer would reveal itself, unfurling elegantly.

Inside was a miniature house, containing a tiny bed with

crumpled covers, a narrow oven with a kettle that never ceased to whistle, a pot of poppies, a recently opened letter, a window with a view to the garden. It had everything, except an equally small person inhabiting it.

Dália understood the problem right away. Matilde had shown her the interior of the drawers on different occasions, and all of them had similar miniatures, woven by Anatema herself. The miniatures moved like they were real, and represented a memory of every bride and maid she had ever devoured. This one lacked the doll representing the deceased.

"That's not all," said Anatema behind her. The creature reminded her of a specter, her hair trickling over Dália's shoulders, her cold breath brushing against the skin of her neck. "After eating her, I reconsidered. She might not have been the thief. Maybe it was someone who knew where the keys were. That's why I called you. I want to know who robbed me."

Dália locked the drawer carefully and descended the ladder.

"How are we going to discover that?"

"We will spend the night in the library, just you and I, little one," Anatema announced. "The door will be closed, and if there is no theft, I will assume the keeper of the keys was innocent, and I will eat you, her apprentice, instead. If there is another theft, I will assume both of you are innocent, and we will need to find the real culprit."

Dália glanced at the stairway out of the corner of her dark eyes. In front of the steps leading to the attic was the last part of the warning:

**LEST THAT YOUR HEART'S BLOOD
SHOULD RUN COLD**

2

Matilde selected Dália from a group of children brought to the house by local orphanages. *The future keeper of the keys,* she had announced proudly, while the others were taken by launderers and cooks and maids. None of them ever moved up from the first floor, even after fifteen years passed. Matilde took her by the hand as they went up the stairs, smiling when the girl gawked at the golden handrails and sculpted arches. *It's just like having a granddaughter.*

Older employees mentored orphans and raised abandoned newborns to pass their knowledge to younger generations. It was part of the rules of the house: those who worked there, lived there, and would die there, one day. Usually, only people who had nowhere else to go chose such a life, but some of the employees provided for entire families with their substantial wages. They rarely mingled with the villagers nearby, and outsiders recognized them for their prideful stances, dark uniforms, and blue ribbons or cravats, expecting them to be as conceited and distant as they looked and acted.

What is she like? Dália had asked when Matilde tucked her into bed that very first night. *Madam is an Archaic One.*

Matilde offered in response an enigmatic smile. *There are very few of them nowadays.*

She remembered imagining a very old woman with a crinkled face, white hair, and sunken eyes. *Once, many Archaic Ones roamed the land,* Matilde had continued, her voice lulling her to sleep. *A long, long time ago . . .* Matilde herself was old, wasn't she? She was well past her sixth decade, but her earthy skin only had two deep lines, and her dark gray hair grew in thick short curls. Only her hands, marked with freckles and bulbous veins, gave away her age.

It doesn't matter what she is. Matilde had caressed Dália's face, gently closing her eyes. *What matters is that you're here.*

"Is it Ms. Matilde?" Dália asked in a whisper.

Anatema nodded, her fake face concentrated and still.

They had been locked in the library for hours. It was late in the night, and Dália had to turn on the electric lamps, since the darkness didn't bother Anatema and she could go on for hours without thinking of light. The owner of the house had been weaving a doll with a familiar look: an elderly woman with a stout body and curly hair, wearing a black suit and an indigo ribbon instead of a tie.

Dália sat by her side to watch her weave. Her stomach growled, reminding her of the time, and Anatema spoke again:

E A T

One of her limbs stretched toward the other desk to remove the crystal lid off a candy jar, grabbing a handful of Turkish delight. Her long fingers stopped centimeters away from Dália's mouth.

"Are you going to create a drawer for Ms. Matilde?"

Dália chose a rosewater candy covered in sugar. "Do you regret eating her?"

Anatema snaked her head closer. Her eyes revealed nothing, as neutral as her closed mouth.

SHE WAS A GOOD KEEPER OF THE KEYS

Dália took another Turkish delight, closing her eyes after swallowing a particularly sweet bit. She supposed she could not expect reasonable explanations from Archaic Ones.

"Is it her bedroom?"

Anatema stopped weaving. One of her arms bent unnaturally behind her back, and she typed a letter. The paper flew, folded, and inserted itself inside a beautiful envelope, disappearing under the door.

MATILDE NEVER TOLD ME ANYTHING

Dália wiped the sugar off her fingers with a napkin. She was frighteningly calm at the possibility of facing death. Maybe because Matilde had prepared her for the idea that they could be eaten at any time, maybe because Matilde herself had met the same fate, as if that was the immutable future of every keeper of the keys.

"I could have delivered the letter to Lionel myself, if you wanted."

NO

YOU STAY HERE

The last words felt like they had been hammered into her chest. Dália knew Anatema had already made up her mind because of the content of the letter, but she failed to understand her fury.

"Of course, madam."

The softness of Dália's answer seemed to calm her down. Anatema looked at her with curiosity, surrounding her with the extending neck, a blue boa constrictor with a human mask.

DO YOU KNOW HOW I MAKE THE MEMORIES?

"The miniatures?" Dália removed a black strand from her own forehead, taking a deep breath to relax her stiff shoulders.

MEMORIES

She shook her head. Dark circles stained her face as the hours passed, and sometimes her eyelids faltered, closing for a few seconds before opening again. Two slices of silver skin unfolded from Anatema's jaw, and part of her mouth opened:

"All the memories I have woven were made out of stories. Extracts of happiness shared by my brides, fragments of my workers' lives, any detail that makes you little creatures what you are." Matilde's miniature spun above Anatema's hand, and the tiny bunch of keys the doll was holding clinked. "This is why I cannot forgive the thief for stealing the memory of my last bride from me."

The last bride had been a girl who lasted three full weeks, more than most, in addition to the many months she had come to the house as a visitor during the courtship. Dália didn't remember her face very well; she only remembered her beautiful dresses and the poppy bouquets she had in her arms whenever she left.

She had been preoccupied with Matilde, who was not acting like herself at the time. The fatigue, Dália supposed, was caused by age; Anatema's whims and desires must have worn her down over time.

"Did Matilde tell you any story?"

"Never," said Anatema with her real voice. "She claimed

to only need her job. So be it, then. She will keep working in her memory, if that's what she liked most."

Dália looked at the miniature forming on the table. It was part of the third floor, with its mint carpet and walls. It even had the painted peacocks, the golden handrails, and the little wooden doors of the treasury.

"She didn't tell me much, either," confessed Dália while a pistachio Turkish delight melted on her tongue. "I think Ms. Matilde lived only for work."

Anatema made a thoughtful sound. In her hands, the silk web turned into architecture and furniture, bringing everything to life while she pulled and twisted the translucent threads.

"I still don't understand. That one memory, in particular . . ." Anatema's hair fell over the miniature, black and silver spreading around the fake green floor. "I don't know why anyone would be interested in it. My treasures are only valuable to me."

"Archaic art is very rare, madam," suggested Dália. "It might have been for money."

"*It might,*" Anatema repeated, and her voice grew shrill and distorted as she said the two words over and over again. "Isn't it suspicious that you even considered that? I wonder what's crossing your head right now. If you're trying to find a way to avoid your fate . . ."

"I would never dare." Dália cracked her neck, finding a more comfortable position on the leather chair. "All my life is here, in the Capricious House. I don't dream of the outside. I only want to keep your keys; that's all that matters for me."

Anatema left the miniature on the desk, and the doll marched across the tiny representation of the corridor.

"We'll see what happens after dawn, but I hope you're being sincere."

Dália observed in silence as the owner of the house finished the memory. Her body ached with hunger and fatigue, but she had learned to control both things. *Never say no to Anatema,* Matilde had taught her. *I never met such a capricious woman.* Sometimes, Dália took small naps, lulled by the soft sound of the cuckoo clock's pendulum.

She stood up with a jump when the automated bird left its home to announce the time: six o'clock.

"Time to discover the truth," said Anatema.

Dália rubbed her eyes and fixed her ribbon. *Time to die,* her mind corrected, but she only nodded quietly.

"Any last words?" The creature left her work aside and straightened her back, her thin torso growing until her head reached the ceiling. Her upper arms fell to her sides like a human being, but the other limbs were on the floor like the spider she was. "I always enjoy giving some time to a person before eating them. Some like to speak. Others pray. If you'd like privacy to cry, I can wait for you outside."

Dália tidied her black suit and dragged the chair back to its place.

"Can I ask you something?"

"Is that your last wish?" Anatema looked amused, curling her neck until her face was almost upside down. "You want to satisfy your curiosity? Be my guest."

"Why do you eat all your brides?" Dália asked. *What a waste of my last minutes of life,* she thought, feeling like an insect paralyzed by the strong venom of a predator. Still, she raised her chin to face Anatema. "I've always wanted to know."

"Why?" Anatema repeated the question, more to herself than to Dália. "Well, it's obvious, isn't it? I hate being seen."

3

The elevator descended slowly, accompanied by a loud mechanical noise. Dália had been granted the right of returning to her bedroom to sleep, but she first had to notify Lionel of the second theft. Although the majordomo acted as Anatema's right hand, only women could go to the third floor, so the two only communicated through notes or the candlestick telephone that connected his room to the library.

His office was the last room of the corridor where turquoise and indigo employees slept: all the maids of the upper floor, the electricians, the butlers, the keeper of the keys. When she knocked, a familiar drawling voice answered immediately:

"Come in."

Dália closed the door behind her. Lionel's eyes went wide, his irises the same shade of light brown as his hair, and he sighed with relief.

"Oh, thank goodness," he finally said, leaving the desk to meet her. The blue tarantula followed him, walking on the table. "That means . . ."

"There was another theft, yes." Dália dropped on the leather armchair, feeling her body relax as her heavy eyelids threatened to shut. She wanted to eat something other than the Turkish delight that Anatema kept pushing toward her, drink a warm cup of poppy tea, and go to sleep. "That also means I'm hired."

"The fact that we have a thief concerns me, of course, but we'll think about this later." Lionel took a hand-painted porcelain kettle from his bureau and poured tea for her. A shrunken red poppy fell over the cup and bloomed atop the hot water. "What matters right now is that you're alive and well."

Dália grabbed a piece of gingerbread dipped in chocolate from the cookie jar near the kettle and sat down again.

"I'm starving."

"I'll tell the kitchen to send breakfast to your room." Lionel sat by her side. He was not a handsome man, with his droopy eyes, aquiline nose, thin downturned mustache, pointy chin, and pale complexion. Actually, he reminded Dália of a reanimated corpse. But there was something charming about his oddness, his longish hair, his wide bony shoulders, and Dália couldn't help a surprised gasp when he took her by the hand. "I already spoke to Anatema, but I want to hear your side as well."

She told him everything she could think about the previous night. That the owner of the house regretted eating Matilde, that she spent the night making a new memory, that they did not leave the library and, when they went to the treasury, the drawer was already open.

"What was it this time?"

"A miniature letter from the last bride," answered Dália. She was disappointed when Lionel pulled his cold fingers away from hers. They reminded her of Anatema's glacial breath, cold as the vapor from the ice boxes where they kept sorbet pots and meat. "I don't think they're related. I think the thief wants to sell Archaic art."

"A reasonable theory," Lionel agreed, petting his tarantula. "A single drawer could provide for at least five generations. But we should not hurry. First, you need to sleep."

Dália protested, but Lionel was so keen on making her rest that he signed a professional order and sealed it with the official seal of the Capricious House. *Dália, keeper of the keys, sleep until 1 PM,* said the note.

It was strange to walk down the same corridor she walked every day as the new keeper of the keys. The sound she had previously associated with Matilde—the jangling keys that announced her presence—now came from the bulk weighing down the tips of her own fingers. One of the maids, a girl her age, offered a vague smile when she heard the sound, and the two exchanged silent nods.

When she reached her bedroom, Dália left her shoes behind the door, hung the bunch of keys on the valet stand, and put on a cotton nightgown. While undoing her hair, she realized something was different in her bedroom: there was a second spider tank, but she was not the one who put it there.

Una, her Chilean rose, was immobile in the corner of her terrarium, while Matilde's spider ate a half-devoured cricket in hers. Dália smiled and covered herself with the duvet.

The warm bed, the smell of mullet croquettes coming from the kitchens, the distant barks of the dalmatians running through the woods—all of it melted together until it became a single continuous thing, embracing her and lulling her to sleep. Dália felt like she was falling, as if there was a cliff under the mattress, and a bottomless river after the cliff. Before she realized, she was back on the third floor, standing behind a folding screen.

Dália touched the blue paper. She could see a feminine silhouette on the other side: straight hair, a hardly visible nose, a long neck, and the hemline of a robe. At the same time, she heard faint voices, talking in the kitchen: *You'll see,* a cook said, and the other agreed, *They always find a way of blaming one of the maids.*

The woman on the other side of the folding screen bobbed her head. There was something uncanny about it, like the undulation of a snake or the rotation of an owl. Dália wanted to look at her, but deep inside she knew it was forbidden. She touched the red key, warm with fresh blood, and waited for the woman to turn her back so she could peek.

What she found was not a person, but a hole: endless and cold, with its walls of turquoise flesh pulsating as she fell, suffocating her, wetting her with saliva, and piercing her with teeth until she was swallowed and dead.

Dália woke up with a jump.

She couldn't remember her dream, but she vaguely recalled the conversation she overheard coming from the kitchen. There was a tray with breakfast at the door and, outside, she saw the caretaker brushing the brilliant coat of a dalmatian. The typewritten note on the plate read:

```
GO TO THE THIRD FLOOR AT DUSK.
```

Lionel appeared with a binder under his arm while Dália was eating lunch. It was already three in the afternoon, which meant the second kitchen was empty. The maids had provided a feast for the owner of the house, the cooks had eaten and washed all the dishes, and all that was left were the breads and cakes in the oven, the cauldrons full of laudanum, and the bottles of opium wine.

The cooks brought Dália a formidable lunch: the same mullet croquettes she smelled in her dream, collard greens, banana farofa, and a portion of deep-fried tarantula. Unfortunately, there was no Turkish delight for dessert.

Dália dipped a crispy spider leg in passion fruit sauce and offered Lionel a bite.

"I already ate," he said, checking the registries.

"Can you see who went to the third floor yesterday?"

"Here . . ." Lionel traced the names, schedules, and occupations. "Branca and Filipa, maids, entered at eleven a.m., left at six p.m. Susana, head chef, delivered lunch at noon and dinner at ten p.m."

"Right, I'll talk to them." Dália swallowed the last crunchy leg and let out a pleased sound. "See you later."

The first suspect was Branca, who was in the garden with other azure maids. She sat on a bench with her skirts lifted, revealing robust white legs, while the sun burned the back of her head as she scored poppy pods with a blade to harvest the milky latex that dripped from them. When the maids noticed Dália, with her black suit and her indigo ribbon, they fled, inventing excuses to work somewhere else. Only Branca remained, unaffected.

"Ms. Branca." Dália sat on the bench next to her. "Can we talk?"

Branca threw the pod she had been working on away; it had streaks of dark brown resin on the surface that looked like red scars. On the other side of the field, gleeful flowers stretched toward the sun in a myriad of colors: bright red, salmon, yellow, orange, purple, white.

"I knew that, at some point, someone would interrogate me." Branca rolled up her sleeves, wiping her hands on the black dress. "Lionel told you to come?"

"Madam Anatema did."

"Well, if it's about Ms. Matilde's death, I didn't see anything. She shouldn't have been there so early in the morning, anyway. Who told her to go? I think Madam Anatema must have been hungry."

Dália looked at Branca. Her rosy skin was tanned from hours under the sun, but it seemed she was still susceptible to its burn; she had red blotches scattered across her cheeks, neck, and shoulders. Her fine hair had been tied into a messy bun, and her fingers bore thin scars caused by the blade she used to harvest latex.

The woman didn't look like any of the exuberant maids of the second floor, who wore white gloves to clean the Capricious House in order to protect their manicured nails, but like someone accustomed to working outside. A replacement.

"Who did you cover for, the day before yesterday?" Dália asked delicately; she didn't want to disrespect her.

"Carla, a turquoise ribbon." Before any other question, Branca added: "Sprained her ankle. Can't work for a month."

"I see. Did you see anything out of place, when you went upstairs?"

Branca smirked. "There's something very strange on the third floor, but we all know what it is, don't we?"

"I'm not speaking of Anatema . . . Not *necessarily*," continued Dália. She wiped the sweat off her face, feeling her cheeks hot with sunlight. "Did you meet the last bride?"

"I've been working there for two or three weeks, so, yes, of course. Unfortunately." Branca narrowed her eyes. "What a brat."

"Brat?"

"Crying all the time. I don't get them, the brides. I don't know how they can cause so much trouble for poor

Madam Anatema," grumbled Branca, covering her blond hair with the azure scarf she pulled from her apron pocket. "It's ridiculous. The woman, if we can call her that, does everything for them. Gives them all the gifts in the world. They live like princesses. Is it that hard to avoid looking at her face?"

Dália opened her mouth to answer, then paused to consider.

"I agree, they also annoy me," she lied. "I think Madam Anatema would not have eaten the last one if she had not disobeyed."

Branca nodded emphatically. "Fools, the whole lot."

"If they didn't disobey, they could be rich beyond belief," Dália kept improvising, the corner of her lips almost curling in satisfaction. "I'm sure that Madam Anatema would weave any kind of treasure, if they only asked."

Branca gazed at the field of poppies. She didn't seem to have any opinion regarding her suggestion.

"She might have, yes, but who knows? Certainly not us; our salaries are more than enough. The same can be said about the brides. The house has everything we need." Branca shrugged, and even smiled. "We just can't disrespect Madam Anatema."

Dália already knew Filipa, who lived in a single bedroom on the second floor. She was a gaunt woman, so cadaverous that she looked like a dried-up branch fallen lifelessly from a winter tree. Her sallow olive skin hugged her bones tightly, defining her protruding cheekbones, her strong nose, her bony fingers, her thin torso.

Every time Dália saw her in the corridors, she looked

absent-minded, lost in a hazy dream that nobody else could see. *It's the flowers,* Lionel told her one day, pointing at Filipa with his chin. *She's a bit too fond of the poppies, if you know what I mean.*

She knew what he meant as soon as she entered Filipa's room.

The maid was lying on her bed, reclined against two goose down pillows. A pipe hung from her mouth, and she held it with gloved hands, still wearing the black suit with a crumpled white apron. At least she had been conscientious enough to remove her unpolished shoes, but otherwise it just looked like she entered and threw herself on her bed.

Dália waved away a puff of sweet-smelling smoke. Filipa slept, unaware of her presence and the burning flame in her cloisonné opium lamp.

"You poor thing," Dália told the brown tarantula, shrunken and feeble in the corner of her terrarium. She opened the tank to help her, but the spider was already dead.

Dália checked all the wardrobes, but she didn't see anything from the last bride's memory. All she found were Filipa's clothes and several paper cards reminding her of the debts she'd collected in the kitchen. Five paregoric elixirs she failed to pay, several slices of poppy seed cake, countless opium balls.

The motive was clear, but Dália didn't feel like Filipa could be the thief. It was hard to believe that the skeletal yet kind Filipa, who roamed the corridors of the third floor with her meticulous duster and peaceful daydreams could have made such a bold move.

Dália removed the pipe from Filipa's lips, turned off the lamp, and took the dead tarantula to the garden. Before returning, she wrote a note in the kitchen: *Please take an afternoon tea to Filipa's bedroom.*

"Dália, my child!" Susana's vivacious voice made her stop in the middle of the stairway. "Can we talk?"

The head chef of the Capricious House was the supreme leader of the kitchens. She instructed the other cooks like a maestra leading her orchestra: inventing menus for Anatema's lavish feasts, writing new recipes, and taking meals upstairs all by herself. She was the only black suit on the first floor, and the one person Anatema trusted with her gastronomic needs.

Dália smiled; she had been searching for her.

"Of course, Ms. Susana." Dália went down the spiral stairs until they were face to face.

Susana was a short and corpulent middle-aged woman, the extreme opposite of Filipa, and her sandy skin was full of lines that came from an elegant hooked nose and ended in a charming mouth. She wore her indigo ribbon around the collar of her shirt, and her dark gray hair was tied into a tall bun.

"See, my dear," said Susana, taking Dália by the arm. "Lionel told me about this thief that caused Matilde's death. Can I help with the investigation in any way? I was the one who found her remains, you know. There wasn't much left, of course. Only blood and shoes."

Dália blinked; if Lionel told her, he must have trusted her as an ally.

"Do you know anyone who could have done something like this?" Dália looked around as she whispered. "I believe the thief must have been after Archaic art."

"Yes, yes, I think so, too. Some girls have opium debts, but I can't believe any of them would have gone so far." Susana sighed, shaking her head. "See, I feel very sorry for Matilde. It's in their nature, you know, the nature of Archaic Ones. We know that. But still . . ."

"It didn't have to happen so soon."

"No, it didn't." Susana took her to the elevator and pressed the button to go to the ground floor. "But it's part of our job! It is, it is. See, sometimes I think that's how I'll bid all of you farewell. Maybe, when I'm older, I'll accidentally speak too fast or too slow, and will end up calling her Madam Ana*the*ma . . ."

Dália smiled and looked at the clock above the door of the elevator.

"I think it's time for me to go."

"Good luck, dear. I'll keep an eye out in the kitchens. Just one more thing!" Susana went to the silver food cart waiting in the corridor. There was a barrel of laudanum, bowls full of peaches in syrup, and several îles flottantes. "Take the food for me, yes?"

4

Dália tried to imagine how the brides must have felt when they first stepped on the carpet of the third floor. The complicated iron arabesques of the elevator, the long Persian rug that came from the lift and continued toward the corridor, the scarlet poppies in their pots, the peacocks painted in the vibrant greenery of the walls. And, ahead, Anatema's endless treasury: door after door, some of them inlaid with intarsia, others with marquetry in marble and mother-of-pearl, their locks coated with gold, the numbers that divided and organized them.

Wherever they looked, they would have been in awe, those bright young women with their expensive dresses. Maybe they were charmed by the sumptuous facade of the Capricious House, or by the pack of well-nurtured dalmatians. Maybe they found the field of ever-living poppies romantic, or maybe they adored the elaborate dishes prepared by the kitchens.

She could even see them, guided by one of the maids. *Good morning, my lady,* Lionel would have said downstairs, as they walked in front of the music room with a gramophone that never stopped playing. *Your wishes are our command.*

All the wonder in the world would not prepare them to find the one who had courted them for months hiding behind a folding screen, nothing but an elongated shadow.

I WAS UNFAIR, KEEPER OF THE KEYS

Anatema was crouching by Dália's side, almost like a human woman. Her false face was solemn, her long legs were folded under her robes, her hair had been combed, and only two arms appeared under her sleeves, retracted near her torso in thoughtful neutrality. Everything appeared normal, except for her immense height, and her incredibly tall neck.

Her silver skin was not the only thing to shine blue under the electric lights. Dália's skin looked purpureous, as if she, too, was trapped in a liminal space, absorbed by the house itself. She glanced at the keys again.

"I'm not sure I follow, madam."

Anatema let out a strangled sound that seemed to come from the pincers in her neck. The way she was standing made her look more like a praying mantis than a spider, and her lower jaw detached from the rest to reveal a sharp laugh.

"I believe I treated you too roughly yesterday. You must understand," continued Anatema with her shrill voice. "I was too upset. I had never been robbed before. During the day, I reflected on my actions and realized I was mistaken."

Dália raised eyebrows; the confession surprised her.

"So?" Anatema's face was near hers. The white chelicerae surfaced like two sharp, marble claws, which Dália supposed was the closest thing she would get to a lighthearted smile. "Do you accept, Miss Dália?"

"Is that an apology?" Dália wanted to laugh, but

Anatema didn't look amused, so she covered her mouth with her hand. "Yes, I do."

The two spent a long while standing in front of the treasury. The owner of the house seemed very content with herself after having "apologized," although, truth be told, she had never uttered the words. Dália smiled. Maybe an accurate reading of Anatema's intentions and coded behavior was part of surviving the third floor.

"So?" Anatema repeated. "Nothing to tell me? If I remember correctly, I gave you a mission before I sent you downstairs."

"I spoke to every employee who came here on the day of the theft, with the exception of Matilde." Dália held the iron ring that kept the keys together with two hands. Before meeting Anatema, she tried one more time to clean the stained key with a brush, but it still looked as red as it did on the first day, like it had been soaked in blood. "Based on what they told me, no one . . ."

AND YOU BELIEVED THEM?

A shiver ran down her spine. Dália dreaded Anatema's other voice, the one that echoed like they were at the bottom of a well.

"Why wouldn't I?"

HUMANS LIE

Again the horrible glacial feeling that made her feel like Anatema herself was freezing her bones.

"Madam," Dália called in a small voice that seemed to surprise Anatema. "Can you speak the other way, please?"

"I don't like to show my teeth," replied the owner of the house. Anatema tried to recoil her imposing size, but there wasn't much she could do to not look absurdly bigger than Dália. "It makes all of you shiver."

Dália didn't ask if "all of you" referred to her workers, to women, to humans. She didn't ask, either, if Anatema's little brides tensed up in fear whenever she stretched her mouth open, or if Matilde had flinched in horror at the sight.

"I don't mind the teeth," Dália pointed out. "And I'm not afraid."

It was true; so far, the world of the third floor was everything she had expected it to be. Even Anatema's mouth was no surprise to her. Potential keepers of the keys were exposed to complex illustrations detailing typical Archaic anatomy, so they would get used to the owner of the house, and Dália felt nothing but curiosity at the sight of her countless fangs, ready to rip her apart.

Anatema was quiet for a couple of seconds.

"Well, well, well . . ." When she started moving toward the treasury, all illusions of humanity disappeared. Her strange locomotion was too eerie, a fact that was even more evident when her impossibly long fingers adhered to the doors effortlessly, allowing her to walk on a vertical surface without climbing it. "Maybe we should check if there was another theft. Open every door. Come, keeper of the keys."

Dália rolled the ladder and unlocked drawer by drawer. Every door hid a secret world: a doll lying under an orange tree, the amaranth-pink bedroom of a baroness, a tiny library with a view to a park, a sapphire necklace hanging from a vanity.

From up close, everything looked real, everything besides the faceless dolls and their stilted movements, too fluid and repetitive to be real.

This one was the daughter of the sculptor who created

monuments for the nearest village, said Anatema, pointing to one of the drawers. *This bride complained all the time.* She spoke of them like she was talking about the furniture of the house. *This one was a pretty sight, but very dull otherwise.* Another drawer, another house. *This one came from a family of carpenters, this one was an ébéniste.*

Dália was especially drawn to the miniature workers. Most of them were keepers, or so she said. *This one was very ill, so I mercifully ate her,* explained Anatema. *This one said her happiest memory was the time her children were alive.* She pointed at the smaller dolls held by a former maid.

With the exception of the last bride, no other piece had been stolen.

After they finished, Anatema poured laudanum into a glass cup and took sips of the dark red beverage. Matilde used to say that the creature drank her laudanum in the beastliest of ways, finishing entire barrels in one gulp. *Even her tongue looks black when she's done!* That time, she had protruded her eyes and grabbed Dália by the shoulders all of a sudden to scare her, laughing when she squealed. *She's not like us; opium causes her no harm.*

Yet Anatema looked composed now, like she was drinking expensive wine.

Dália went back to the last bride's drawer. There was nothing unusual this time—the bed was still a mess, the table continued there, the kettle kept whistling. With her finger, Dália straightened the duvet and opened the fake window.

"I don't really remember her," admitted Dália, sitting on a step. Her memories of the bride were vague, and she did not even remember her name; there were so many brides, after all. "Why do you think the thief focused on her?"

Anatema stretched her neck until she was in front of the drawer, but her body was far from her.

"It might be a coincidence. This room is my least valuable treasure. Even less valuable than the memories of the maids." Her face, pale and still, stared at the room. "My little traitor had nothing to her name. Even her mother, the only family she had, died weeks before our wedding. And still, she betrayed me. I, the only one who would take care of her."

If she tried hard enough, Dália could conjure the image of the last bride from behind, walking to the elevator. Her orange dress, her walnut waves, her lean back.

"Traitor?"

"Twice a traitor," confirmed Anatema. Her serrated pincers clicked while she spoke. "First, because she insisted on looking at me. Second, for being unfaithful."

Dália waited, and Anatema glanced at her out of the corner of her cobalt eyes.

"Remember the letter in her room?" She pointed at the miniature with one of her three long fingers. "She received those every month. Never signed, always with money, but, and I'm quoting her, she knew they were written by someone who loved her."

WHICH IS RIDICULOUS
WHY WOULD SHE CARE,
IF I, TOO, COULD LOVE HER?

Anatema's disembodied voice nauseated Dália. She lowered her head, facing the bride's tiny table, where the envelope had been.

"She had no idea who could have sent those letters?"

SHE BELIEVED THEY WERE FROM THE
FATHER WHO ABANDONED HER

Dália's nose touched the little diorama as she examined it. Nothing strange except three black hairs under the duvet. She pressed her thumb on the drawer's floor and looked at what seemed like a trio of extremely thin eyelashes.

"Well, madam," said Dália. "I think we found our first clue."

5

Few were the people who could brag about having encountered an Archaic One. The creatures were as old as the world itself, and their gargantuan bodies did not obey the same laws as the living beings who surrounded them. Their limbs bent at unthinkable angles, and countless appendages sprouted from them as fangs, eyes, chelicerae, wings, and claws.

Dália had heard of Archaic Ones whose skins were inside out: instead of faces, they were covered by dentate gum with protruding marble. Another Archaic One had an annelid body that extended for miles and, although it reminded humans of an eel because of its shape and ability to generate electricity, it gnawed rocks in caves and could not touch water.

Compared to her strange siblings, Anatema was humanlike. Nothing like the Archaic Ones who spoke only through enigmas, or whose venom boiled the ground they touched; the owner of the Capricious House was surprisingly normal. She enjoyed the company of humans (when she did not devour them), she lived in society (somewhat), she was able to hold entire conversations (when she felt like it).

Why would anyone steal from an Archaic One? Dália

analyzed the hairs with the magnifying glass she found in the library, but she was not even close to a productive answer. They could belong to anyone. She even compared the samples to her own eyelashes, but the ones above her cheeks were longer, thicker, and darker.

From her three initial suspects, Branca had naturally blond eyelashes, but they could have belonged to Filipa or Susana. *And to most people in the house.*

Dália took the lashes with tweezers and placed them inside a small flask. If she shared any of her thoughts with Anatema, the Archaic One would reach an extreme conclusion: eat everyone with dark eyelashes, including Dália. Maybe she would leave the men alone, since they did not have permission to reach the third floor, but most of the women would be ingested by the end of the day.

"Madam," called Dália, walking down the corridor. She didn't know where Anatema was. "Madam!"

She checked every single room on the third floor, all with the same nefarious warning in front of the door:

BE BOLD, BUT NOT TOO BOLD

The recreation room, the boudoir, the back terrace, the bathrooms, the art gallery . . . Anatema was nowhere to be found.

Dália stopped in front of a pot of poppies next to the staircase. How would she find her if she could not go to the attic? A swish of wind blew against her face, and Dália looked around, only to discover the window was closed. Wind . . . ?

THAT WAS GREAT FUN,

KEEPER OF THE KEYS

Dália jumped at the sound. She turned around to find Anatema behind her, wearing a pitch-black robe. Her silver skin mask smiled slightly, and her bicolored hair fell on her neck in fluid stripes.

"I did not see you coming, madam."

Anatema looked at the ceiling and her fake mouth stretched into a cynical grin.

I didn't look up, Dália scolded herself. *How silly of me.*

"You must have needed me, screaming so desperately . . ."

She ignored the mockery.

"Yes, I need to check something. May I?" Dália bit her inner lip. Maybe Anatema would find the idea offensive, but she wanted to discard every possibility. "It's a little invasive."

Anatema blinked with curiosity. When she nodded, Dália climbed several steps, until they were close enough in height. *Here, here,* she called, and Anatema went up the vertical surface of the elevator effortlessly. Her neck went toward Dália, and the two were face to face.

"It might hurt, but bear with me," warned Dália.

She placed one hand on Anatema's pale cheek to hold her still and took the tweezers from the pocket of her pants. Anatema observed her in silence, but she seemed amused, at least. Up close, the mimicry was even more evident. Her eyes had no pupil or color gradient, displaying, instead, the toxic and metallic intensity of a blue poison dart frog.

Dália pulled one of Anatema's lashes with the tweezers, and the creature flinched.

"I told you it could hurt," argued Dália before she could complain. She lifted the tweezers against the light and compared her eyelashes to the ones in the vessel.

They were definitely different.

"So?" Anatema's neck undulated until her head was upside down. The lines around her mouth lifted slightly, showing the side fangs when she smiled.

"I think yours is silver." The eyelash was on her thumb,

and Dália blew it away to make a wish: *let me find the culprit before anyone else ends up dead.*

"If you had asked me, I could have told you that."

"It didn't hurt to try." Dália went down the stairs and stepped on the words engraved in front of the stairway:

**LEST THAT YOUR HEART'S BLOOD
SHOULD RUN COLD.**

"I will speak to Lionel. Maybe he can give me an idea."

BUT DON'T FORGET . . .

Dália turned around, one hand stiff on the elevator door. She thought Anatema would use again the horrible disembodied voice, but she finished with her normal tone:

"Be back for dinner."

Dália went to Lionel's room, unsure where to start the investigation. The majordomo had finished the working schedule for next week, and he was sitting behind the desk, sealing letters. He coated the back of every stamp with glue, closed the envelopes, and left them in a neat pile, while Minerva, his cobalt blue tarantula, walked on his arms.

"It really is a problem," Lionel agreed without looking at Dália. Minerva stopped on the back of his hand when he left the stamps aside. "Maybe you should focus on another clue. You can't check the eyelashes of every single person in the house."

"At least I know something. It wasn't Branca or Anatema herself." Dália laid her cheek and arm on the desk, petting Minerva. The spider's legs, pedipalps, chelicerae, and thorax were mostly covered by the same particular blue shade, with the exception of some black, white, and yellow sprinkled here and there. "I don't know what to do. I'm afraid that if she grows too impatient, she will eat everyone and call it a day."

"At best, she might forget it like it never happened; at worst, she will choose a random culprit, nothing else." Lionel also caressed the spider. After a few moments of silence, he looked at Dália with a grin. "Do you want to check mine? Maybe if you see another person's lashes you will feel more productive."

Dália smiled back. She could see from there that Lionel was not the one, but she still got up to hold his face like she had done with Anatema.

Under the light, Lionel's violet veins were visible behind the eyelids, and gray strands sprinkled his brown hair. Dália compared the vessel with his lashes. Again, it was too light.

"I feel like I'm missing something obvious . . ." When Lionel blinked, his eyelashes brushed the tips of her fingers, and Dália giggled. "Probably nothing important."

She was still smiling when her gaze found a pile of letters, reminding her of the stolen item. Dália took an envelope and traced the address.

"Dália?"

"What are those?" Dália checked several letters, but none of them looked anything but professional.

"It's just Anatema's business." Lionel frowned. "Receipts of sales of paregoric elixir, lists of groceries, deliveries, bills from the last wedding . . ."

"Anything belonging to the last bride?"

Lionel raised an eyebrow.

"Why would we have that?" He left Minerva on the desk to point at the blue wax of the Capricious House. "Only finances."

"I thought . . ." Dália bit her lower lip, following the

spider with her eyes. "Do you still have the address of her family?"

"All her family is dead. Besides, why do you think the thefts have anything to do with her, specifically?"

Dália stood up. "I don't know. I need to think."

LATE

was the first thing Dália heard when she reached the third floor. She began to open the iron gate of the elevator when Anatema's haunting voice resounded inside her chest. The gust of wind had been so strong she had to hold on to the handrail to avoid falling down, and the bunch of keys rattled under her fingers.

At first, Dália did not understand the accusation. Only when she lifted her face did she see the trail of sweets left on the red carpet, leading to the corridor. The first was a single profiterole, left on an embellished napkin near the inscription of

BE BOLD, BE BOLD.

"Madam?"

No answer.

Dália took a bite of the cream puff powdered in sugar. The trail continued far from the treasury, with several other desserts left along the way. Luckily, one of the maids had thought ahead and left a wicker basket by the elevator, as if urging her to collect them.

"Madam," Dália called again. She followed the sweet tracks like a child in an Easter game.

Besides the profiterole, she found an empanada with bittersweet tarantula filling, a cherry of the Rio Grande–

flavored petit four, a trout roll, a dulce de leche pionono. Dália placed everything inside the basket with care, trying to preserve the pistachio halvas, the marzipan spiders, the tartlets covered with ripe pitangas.

She retrieved them one by one, until she arrived in the dining room, greeted by the same warning she saw every day:

BE BOLD, BUT NOT TOO BOLD.

Dália gasped when she saw what awaited her.

Instead of a table, the feast had been organized on the floor, over a turquoise mat. Blue poppy pots had been arranged throughout the room, and the dishes were varied: stuffed armadillo, swallow tartare, cashew nut rice, deep-fried tarantulas, tiramisu.... There was so much food that nearly all the floor was covered with plates and bowls—enough to feed every worker in the Capricious House.

Across the room was a blue folding screen, and she could see a woman's shadow behind it.

"Late," repeated Anatema, hidden by the furniture. The outline of her black-and-silver hair moved as if blown by the wind. "The food is getting cold."

"Are we waiting for someone?" Dália asked, leaving the basket on the floor.

Anatema huffed. "Only little Miss Dália."

"Me?" Dália repressed an amused smile. Anatema not only had failed to *invite* her for dinner, but the food was excessive for a dinner for two.

SIT DOWN, SILLY ONE

The order made her fall to her knees. Dália blinked, staring at Anatema's floating head, trying to understand how she had forced her to sit down like that. She decided against questioning her, as it would be pointless, and left the heavy bunch of keys aside.

"I'm honored, madam." Dália massaged the palm of her right hand. Holding the keys for long periods of time left her skin bruised, and her wrist and elbow twitched in pain. "Won't you come eat with me?"

Anatema nodded before hiding again.

Dália sat on a pillow. In front of her was a plate with a huge Goliath birdeater fritter adorned with flowers like an edible bouquet. Behind the folding screen, Anatema looked restless.

"Help yourself, then turn around and face the door," she ordered. "And don't peek."

"The door?"

I JUST SAID THAT, DIDN'T I?

Dália tried a spoonful of several different courses, along with a deep-fried spider, her favorite homemade dish. She poured herself a glass of strawberry guava soda and turned around.

Something started to move behind her back. Dália glanced at the display cabinet, where she saw the reflection of Anatema's eight legs coming from the folding screen. The Archaic One climbed the walls and moved quickly toward the feast.

A guttural and primordial sound took over the room when her gaping mouth devoured dish after dish. *All of it?* she had asked Susana in the past, whenever she stopped by the second floor with several food trays. *The owner of the house has a marvelous appetite,* the head chef had answered with a smirk.

Now she understood. The quantity of food was not a miscalculation, but a normal intake for Anatema, who consumed everything in sight. Dália lowered her head. She kept peering at the reflection from the corner of her eye, watching with fascinated curiosity as more and more food disappeared. She felt no repulsion or horror at the sight; it would be foolish to expect human manners coming from *her*.

"Would you like a second helping?" Anatema asked over her shoulder, and her freezing breath engulfed Dália.

"I'm done, thank you." Dália smiled and showed her the almost empty plate. Anatema's blue tongue extended to grab one of the tarantula legs she had left behind and went back to her mouth in a second. "If you want more, I can call the kitchen."

NO
GUESTS DON'T WORK

Once again, Dália imagined how the brides must have felt. They did not even know that their suitor was an Archaic One, but were forced to eat facing the door, wondering what kind of hideous secret the owner of the house must have been hiding behind the screen. Perhaps Anatema ate more gracefully during the courtship period. Perhaps the boldest brides spied over their shoulders and never had the chance to even conclude their engagement.

Not that it mattered to the employees. They understood her nature, or at least, they respected it. It would be strange if a creature of her size barely ate, or if Anatema's enormous fingers were able to hold a delicate silver fork.

What really surprised Dália was that she was being treated as a guest.

"If I had known you were inviting me, I would have worn something more appropriate, not my uniform," Dália commented playfully. Her soft laugh replaced the uncomfortable silence, and Anatema moved behind her, curious. "It looks like I have no manners, coming like this."

"Uniform," echoed Anatema. "Uniform, yes, of course. How did I forget about this? I should have sent you a dress."

"It was a jest." Dália tried to turn around. "May I?"

YES

The dining room looked like it had been devastated by a hurricane. Bowls had been turned over, petals and grains had been scattered, and at least one chunk of porcelain had been bitten and devoured. At first glance, Anatema was not moving, but two of her arms collected the remains and threw the trash inside the colorful mat to make things easier for the maids.

MISS

DÁLIA

Dália blinked. Her voice, less of a sound and more like the brusque strength of an earthquake, did not knock her down this time. Anatema mastered herself again to look like a human woman, within the bounds of possibility. Her limbs hid once more under her dark velvet robes, her neck retracted to a nearly believable length, and her inky eyes studied Dália, always immobile.

The lines of Anatema's mouth crooked into a strange smile.

"Tell me more about your life," asked Anatema, the ghostly hiss of her voice lowering to a contained timbre. "How are your days? Are you content with your accommodations? With the company?"

"Well . . ." Sitting on her own heels, Dália wondered if Matilde had gone through this kind of interrogation as well. She could not picture the old keeper of the keys having dinner with Anatema and chatting about her life and prospects. In her imagination, Matilde was always dutiful, holding the bunch of keys, ready to open another drawer. "I don't know what to say, madam."

TRY.

HOW DID YOU GET HERE?

Nobody had ever asked about her life; as a rule, those who worked in the Capricious House only existed within the internal universe of the house.

"Like many other employees, I came here as a child. I was taken from the same orphanage as Elisa and Josefina, who work in the kitchens, and Bento, one of the gardeners," said Dália, her index finger accompanying her explanation, as if she was citing item by item. "Miss Matilde chose me to be her apprentice on my very first day."

DO YOU LIKE YOUR OCCUPATION?

"It's my life. It's all I know," continued Dália. A discreet arm escaped from the sleeve of the velvet robes to reach the telephone and type a code for the kitchens. "Maybe I'm saying this because I'm used to it—but I wouldn't change it for anything in the world."

COMFORT, YES
BUT YOU DIDN'T ANSWER
MY QUESTION,
MISS

"Madam, please, it's very hard for us humans to get used to this voice of yours." Her head throbbed, and Anatema seemed delighted in having caused her to almost faint. "Can you use your vocal cords?"

"I want to know, miss, or Dália, however you want me to call you . . ." Her lips cracked into a dry cut, and the tips of her chelicerae invaded her mocking smile. "If you like it, and if you don't, what do you like? What do you wish for?"

The indigo gleam that went from Anatema's neckline to her jaw mixed with the silvery skin of her face under the ceiling lights. Her head twisted in an impossible angle, and her eyes narrowed into slits that were as blue as her throat and tongue.

"What do *I* wish for?" Dália frowned. Sometimes, she had a fancy or two. Silly ideas came to her mind when she had nothing better to do, thinking of a dish that was not part of the day's menu, or skipping work to spend the afternoon reading in her bed. There were also other desires, more intimate in nature, but she would rather not think of them. "I like to have the safety of a job. I like to eat deep-fried tarantulas every other day. I like . . ."

"No, no, you little fool . . ." One of Anatema's arms appeared under her sleeve, and a single finger touched Dália's indiscernible laryngeal prominence, pressing enough to make her breathless. "What do you *really* want? I can give it to you, if you tell me."

Dália gasped her response: "Why?"

"I like to know what you little people think." Her glee became even more apparent, and Dália realized Anatema was dangerously close to her. Not only that, but she had stopped trying to pretend to be smaller and less unusual, and now she looked like a colossal apparition in front of her eyes. "It amuses me."

Before Dália could answer, someone knocked on the door. Filipa entered the dining room with a silver tray in hand. She had not changed much since the last time Dália saw her, other than being awake this time. Her opaque face looked like a death mask with an eternally distant smile, and her brown eyes were almost closed.

"Dessert for miss Dália," hummed Filipa, leaving the dish in front of her. "Enjoy your meal!"

The maid removed the cloche of the tray to reveal an extravagant dessert: the perfectly preserved white flower of a water lily powdered with castor sugar. The petals were oddly firm, and guava jam dripped from the middle to the plate. Filipa closed the door after she left.

"Try it." Anatema pulled one of the petals that had acquired a gelatin-like consistency. She dipped the flower in the jam and took it to Dália's lips. "This recipe was created here in the house."

The petal dissolved in her mouth, and the sweetness of the smell left her intoxicated for a moment.

"What about Madam Anatema?" Dália took another delicious bite, wiping a drop of jam off her lower lip. "What do you wish for?"

I HAVE EVERYTHING I WANT WHY WOULD YOU THINK THAT I LACK SOMETHING, ANYTHING AT ALL?

Dália felt like laughing at the silly, obvious lie.

"How come? If you did not wish for anything, you wouldn't search for a bride for so many years." She plucked another petal from the dessert. "Nor would you devour them all."

Anatema bristled, abandoning her humanoid posture to fall onto her first four legs, her wide eyes contrasting with her still-smiling mouth.

I THINK YOU HAVE FORGOTTEN SOMETHING, DÁLIA

One of her pointy hands took Dália by the face and forced her to look at the door that opened with the wind. On the floor, the words said:

BE BOLD, BUT NOT TOO BOLD

6

Dália was still thinking of Anatema's warning when she woke up. She had been dismissed after dinner, and the short moment of fury was forgotten. *Come tomorrow again,* the owner of the house said like nothing had happened. But Dália was not worried about Anatema's temper tantrums. The question kept hovering in her mind: *What do you* really *want?*

She tried to come up with an answer to no avail. Maybe she did not want anything at all. She had never learned how to want; she had simply existed, until then. Her life was just a series of routines. At best, she could imagine what she did not want: dying, losing her job, starving, suffering. She did not want inconveniences. She did not want changes. She did not want.

Dália arranged her hair, tying it with the new ribbon. Her desires were limited to short-term wishes. Since last week, she had been thinking about solving a mystery. She noticed, too, that she enjoyed Anatema's company. Yes, she was strange and volatile, but she was never monotonous: Anatema always had a story to tell, and Dália appreciated their differences.

Before leaving, she left crickets for her tarantula, Una,

and Matilde's tarantula, whose name she still didn't know. *Bon appétit,* she told them, closing the door.

In the corridor, with the keys clanking by her side, Dália heard muffled giggles when she walked past two younger maids. They were wiping the floor of the residential wing, and they covered their mouths to hide grins when she turned to see them, which puzzled her.

"Good morning," said Dália out loud, and the maids giggled again.

She decided to ignore it, thinking it must have been some infantile joke. Heading toward the elevator, she came to a halt only when someone yelled her name from the other side of the corridor.

"Dália!" Lionel ran with a binder under his arm. "Dália!"

When he reached her, the man leaned against a pillar, panting. His brown hair was much lighter than the mahogany of the elevator, and his black suit was slightly crumpled.

"Is there anything wrong?"

"I searched for you everywhere. I went to the kitchens, but the cooks told me you asked them to send breakfast to your room, then I went to your room, but you had already left. . . ." Lionel made another pause to breathe. "Where are you going?"

"To the third floor," Dália replied like it was obvious. "Where else?"

"Isn't it too early?"

"Anatema told one of the butlers she needs me right now."

Lionel made a face. His light eyebrows met in the middle, and he closed the metallic gate Dália had half-opened before he reached her.

"I found something you were looking for." Lionel showed her the binder. "Cecília's father."

"Cecília?"

"The last bride."

Dália leafed through the binder as he spoke.

"He works in a nearby village," continued Lionel. "But he will only be there today until one in the afternoon. If you leave now, maybe . . ."

"Madam Anatema won't be too happy about it."

Lionel smiled playfully. Despite being older than her, he was the closest thing to a friend she had in the house.

"I'll deal with that for you. You'll find some money inside the binder, and I asked one of my apprentices to take the car out of the garage."

Dália smiled back, hugging the binder. Maybe she would get her wish sooner than she expected.

The trip was uneventful. The automobile was a perfectly polished blue Model T, and the apprentice unfolded the roof to protect her from the sunlight. They took the forest road in silence, leaving behind the poppy fields until the outline of the house disappeared. Branches framed the path, and Dália stretched to see the landscape. The vehicle only had a front glass window; the sides were open, allowing her to enjoy the view.

Don't be afraid, Matilde had told her when they made the same trip together, countless years ago. The keeper of the keys had decided to take her to town, since Dália was ten and curious to see the world that existed outside the Capricious House.

The experience was an utter failure. Dália spent most of the time hiding behind Matilde, who had fits of laughter whenever someone spoke to them, and Dália pressed her small face against her back, pulling the jacket of her suit.

You're tickling me! Matilde had laughed while they waited in the post office. *Be a good girl!*

Dália was no longer afraid. Excitement bubbled inside her chest whenever she thought of returning with good news, and she observed the dense trees of the forest with detached curiosity. She neither missed the village, nor feared it.

"I'll be right here, miss," said the apprentice, a shy teenage boy who could barely talk to her without stammering. "If you need me . . ."

"I'll call you, thank you."

He parked the automobile near the marketplace. The broad streets of the village were empty, and the few people around stared at the employees of the Capricious House, easily recognizable by their black uniforms and blue ribbons. They were also curious about the car, since very few people in the region owned such vehicles.

According to the binder, Cecília's father delivered fish every week to the butcher shop. Hanged sheep and skinned pigs adorned the entrance, and a child painted a large sign: SALE—SEAFOOD—SALMON—TROUT—MULLET! Inside, a robust man took fish out of an ice box. When he noticed Dália standing next to him, he left the fresh trout aside, its glassy eyes looking pale and yellowish.

"Are you the one who wanted to talk about Cecília?"

"Yes, sir. We are very sorry for your—"

"I wasn't close to my daughter," the man interrupted. "Keep your condolences for those who need them."

Dália was stunned by his indifferent response. She wished Lionel or Matilde were there; they would certainly know how to talk to someone outside of the house.

"Actually, I wanted to ask you about the mail she received," said Dália, growing more nervous as she spoke. "If the letters are yours, we can . . ."

"Oh, the letters? No, they ain't mine. After I remarried, I saw the girl only once or twice. But she already received those back then," added Cecília's father. "Always. We thought they were from an admirer, you know. She was a pretty thing. Maybe the poor soul doesn't even know she's already dead."

If the letters had been written by a young man in town, it wouldn't make a difference in her investigation. Dália left the shop, and the apprentice opened the door, observing her from the corner of his eye.

"Do we need to go somewhere else, miss?"

"No, I'm finished."

The trip back was even quieter than the one before. If she had only been able to read the content of the letters, she might have found a clue or two. Maybe then she would be closer to her true wishes, or closer to solving Cecília's mystery, anyway.

The colorful houses of the village vanished in the background, and they entered the dark forest. Dália remembered the nights she had spent sealing letters with Matilde. *A keeper of the keys never leaves the locksmith,* she used to say, always with a high-spirited smile. Dália was still little, and she helped her by stamping the envelopes with Anatema's sapphire crest. *What about this one?* she had asked. *This one is a little secret.*

Years later, she finally discovered Matilde's secret: she exchanged letters with a former lover from her past life. Dália had been thirteen when she confessed the truth, right after Lionel caught her sending a furtive note. *Well, now you know that even the employees of the Capricious*

House are sentimental, Matilde had laughed, and the bunch of keys tinkled by her side. *You will understand when you grow up.*

Unfortunately, the bride's letters were not available for her current investigation. Lionel showed her the content of the envelopes lying about his desk, but everything was strictly professional, and the few letters mentioning brides spoke of dowries and life insurances for their families.

Dália realized they were already back at the Capricious House, the apprentice waiting outside her door with an extended hand. Dália thanked him for the help, leaping to the ground, and went to the stairway of the first floor, deep in thought. Susana and another cook left the elevator, and the head chef waved when she saw her.

"Did you like the dessert I prepared for you yesterday?" Her smile was friendly and wide. Her magenta lipstick stained her front tooth, and her pristine white gloves held the handles of a food cart.

"It was delicious, Miss Susana."

The younger cook covered a giggle and fled to the kitchen.

"We've just started the menu for today's dinner, do you have any preference? Madam Anatema is not very thoughtful in her whims; for her, you would just eat the most extravagant delicacies . . ."

"I'm having dinner with her again?"

"Didn't she tell you?" Susana raised an eyebrow. "Well, think of it, or I'll choose the dishes myself, yes?"

Dália said, "Yes, choose them for me," feeling even more confused than before. Everyone in the house seemed to orbit around her, or at least observe her in some way. She did not understand. Working in the Capricious House meant mastering the art of being invisible. But, from one day to the next, every other employee seemed suddenly aware that there was a Dália. Was it only because she had assumed the role of keeper of the keys? Or . . . ?

"Miss Dália . . ." Filipa repeated her name several times in a sleepy yet singsong voice. Dália turned around. The two of them bumped into each other in the corridor, and Filipa chuckled, delighted. Despite the maid's spectral appearance, they were actually similar in age, a fact that became more apparent when Filipa laughed holding her own belly. "Calm down, calm down! I'm not going to devour you."

"*Devour?*" Dália felt like passing out. The smell of opium trailed after Filipa, and she felt dizzy, reconsidering every interaction she'd had in the previous hours.

"Look, I even brought you a little gift . . ." Filipa hooked her arm with hers, guiding her toward Dália's bedroom.

On the bed was a beautiful cream-colored dress facing the two spider tanks. Una moved curiously between the rocks of her enclosure, looking like a small pink cloud made of hair. Matilde's tarantula, a Brazilian black, spun her web against the glass, ignoring the women walking around.

"A little gift from the mistress." Filipa sat on a corner of Dália's bed. The mattress jiggled, and the maid's grin only grew. "Will we have a new bride soon?"

"She didn't mention any bride." Dália sat on the other side of the bed. She touched the flowing fabric of the dress, unused to the softness.

"I'm talking about you, silly!"

Dália frowned. "Nonsense."

"It's what everyone in the house is talking about," said Filipa, humming again, her eyes lost somewhere in the wallpaper. "You will wear the dress tonight, right? I can come here and help you get ready."

Dália realized she was trembling. She was unsure if it was fear, since Anatema's attention usually led women to their premature deaths, or if it was the same sensation that followed her through the house after feeling seen for the first time.

"No," she finally said, pushing the dress aside. "I'll wear my uniform, like always."

At night, Filipa came anyway. She did not insist that Dália wear the dress, but she talked her into wearing a black A-line skirt, spraying the same sweet perfume the brides always wore and tying a tiny bow around her short ponytail.

"There, you're looking lovely." Filipa buckled her doll shoes. The two had agreed that wearing heels would be a terrible idea. "You know it's no good to upset Madam Anatema."

Filipa laid the cream-colored dress on the armchair next to the window, the shadow of a reclined woman in the dim light. When someone knocked on the door, Dália almost jumped, startled, and Filipa answered for her.

"What . . . ?" The maid stopped talking. "Oh, good evening, Mr. Lionel!"

"I will handle the rest."

Filipa left the bedroom without a word, and Lionel regarded Dália from the door. She pretended to look at the tanks, again feeling exposed by the constant scrutiny.

"Anatema told me to escort you," answered Lionel. "What's wrong?"

"I always go there alone."

"Not today, evidently." Lionel offered his skinny arm after they left the room. Dália closed the door behind her and hugged his arm, her cheek against his sleeve. "You know, Dália, Matilde and I spoke several times about the day you would succeed her as the keeper of the keys."

"You and Matilde? Why?"

The corners of Lionel's mouth tilted upward under his mustache.

"Both of us shared a certain... *apprehension*... regarding your upcoming meeting with Anatema." The majordomo paused, walking so slowly down the corridor that it felt like they would never reach the elevator. "Of course, you are extremely well prepared. You are clever and attentive. We knew that."

"I don't understand...."

Lionel focused his gaze on the embellished iron gate at the end of the straight path.

"Anatema cannot resist a beautiful woman. That's why we have exuberant engagements every year, isn't it? She is also an Archaic One. Understanding, waiting, and forgiving do not come naturally to her. Anatema kills what she does not like. And, as we know, she kills what she loves, too."

They faced each other in front of the gates. Dália could not tell what Lionel was thinking. He took one of the blue poppies from the pot next to the elevator and pinned it to her lapel.

"I would not like to see you dead," admitted Lionel. "We are taught to lose and mourn from an early age, but none of us wanted this for you. Matilde hoped to give you a good life, when she adopted you."

That being said, the majordomo pulled the lever and closed the doors, and the elevator ascended with the keeper of the keys inside it.

Dália looked at herself in the mirror. It was not the first time she had seen herself. She knew her eyes were black, small, upturned. She knew her nose was medium-sized, that the bridge was flat and discreet, that the tip was round. She knew she had full lips and, when she smiled, part of her white teeth appeared.

She could keep going for hours: her eyebrows were arched, her face oval, her forehead tall. Her hair fell to her shoulders in soft spirals on the rare occasion she did not tie it up, her skin was smooth, her height was average. She was almost thin, in the sense that her collarbone was well-defined, and the round bones of her shoulders and knuckles were apparent.

She knew what she looked like.

She knew, but she did not see. The shape of her face meant nothing to her. She had no opinions regarding the curve of her hip or the width of her waist. Whenever she looked in a mirror, she only saw Dália. Not adjectives, nothing. Only Dália. Wasn't that how everybody else felt?

The elevator arrived on the third floor. There was a small typewritten note in front of the grate, over a stand of sheet music:

GO TO THE ATTIC.

Dália closed the iron door. The elevator would not take her to the attic of the Capricious House, as the only way to access it was through the last flight of stairs. She stepped on the ominous phrase—

**LEST THAT YOUR HEART'S BLOOD
SHOULD RUN COLD**

—and climbed step by step, one hand holding the hem of her skirt and the other on the handrail.

She did not know what to expect when she unlocked the door. A spider's lair, perhaps, dark and nefarious, with webs everywhere, just like the tank of Matilde's tarantula. Instead, she found a maze of folding screens.

"Madam?" called Dália, and her voice echoed in the attic. The ceiling was huge and funneled, covered by complex webs of translucent silk, and the chimney continued toward the roof.

**WAITING FOR YOU ON THE TERRACE,
D
 Á
   L
     I
       A**

There were all kinds of folding screens everywhere she went: lacquered Coromandel, painted butterflies resting on rainbow pinks, calligraphy, and flowing fabrics. Anatema had a collection of screens bought from Chinese merchants, but she also owned gilded Japanese byōbu that formed narrow corridors in her chambers, and some Austrian models as well.

Finally, she found an open door that led to the terrace at the back of the house.

The night was clear and pleasant, and only a few clouds covered the twinkling stars. Dália shivered as she sat on the empty chair, candles flickering in the candelabrum in the middle of the table.

"Are you going to keep hiding, madam?"

A moment of silence followed the question, and Anatema's screeching voice filled her ears, like a knife scratching a metal tray.

"You did not wear my gift." The words came like a breath against Dália's nape, sending goose bumps down her back. Dália tried to turn around, but Anatema stopped her, grabbing her neck with three long fingers. "I didn't say you could look, silly."

The pressure made her gulp. When she thought she would choke, breathless, Anatema released her, letting go of her fingers one by one.

"You're not planning to hide from me, are you?" Dália rubbed her throat over the collar of her white shirt. "I already saw your face, Madam Anatema."

That seemed to bother her. Anatema went to the other side of the table with her arachnid walk, her eight legs moving at the same time. When she sat down, she almost looked like a regular woman, if you ignored that she was not sitting on her chair, preferring to retract anatomically instead.

Again, Dália felt seen.

Anatema's eyes did not move, but she knew they were following her every breath, landing on her figure like the painted butterflies of her folding screens. They were both curious and ravenous, inspecting every part of her, from her fingernails to the shoulders of the suit, her neck, face, hair, chest. They stopped at each centimeter of exposed skin, gluing to her joints and dissecting her limbs.

Had Anatema always looked at her like this, and Dália simply failed to notice? If she had, why wasn't she disturbed by it? Perhaps that was the problem: she found comfort in Anatema's gaze and failed to reject her strangeness. Lionel was right about her nature. Still, Dália felt nothing but fascination for the elongated limbs, the hidden teeth, the faux face.

Across the table, Anatema stretched an arm to remove the cloche from the dish in front of Dália. Inside was the menu Susana had promised, a considerably more reasonable combination than the absurd quantity expected by the owner of the house.

Dália tried the steak with pomegranate sauce, popping sarcotestas with her fork and watching as the red juice dripped down the meat. Anatema started to eat, this time in front of her. Her mouth expanded completely, from the upper jaw to the middle of her neck, broad enough to fit an entire human. The food disappeared in a second between the fangs and chelicerae, swallowed by the interior of her blue larynx.

When they moved to dessert, she couldn't help but ask:

"Is there a reason?" Dália pointed at her. "To hide like this?"

Anatema, whose mouth closed as she thought, made a thoughtful sound.

"A reason? Why, isn't it obvious?" The fake lips distorted in a puckered smile. "My little brides try their best, but despite all their politeness, they end their short lives with horror plastered all over their faces. That is why they must not look. They do not understand."

"I suppose you have a point. . . ." Dália took a spoonful

of tiramisu to her mouth. "But, if you tried to tell them instead of hiding, maybe . . ."

"Maybe, maybe, it's easier said than done. The fact is, I do not exist. Or better: I should not continue to exist." Anatema poured a bottle of laudanum into a crystal glass. "Things are not what they used to be. Those like me are vanishing. And, among you, little people, I see how repulsive I am."

"Some people understand," insisted Dália. "Here in the house, for example . . ."

"What about the house? I'm well aware of how different I am from your four little limbs. My voice hurts you; my movements paralyze you. Sometimes, it amuses me. But when it's a bride, someone I thought I could trust . . ."

"I find it sad." The keeper of the keys set aside the dessert bowl. "It's sad that you feel this way, and sadder still that you're always after a bride, but you never really marry them. Not for more than a few days."

SAD

repeated Anatema.

"I can't speak for your future bride, but please don't hide when you request my presence. I have already seen you," added Dália, staring into her dark blue eyes. "I feel no horror, nor fear, no disgust. Eat whenever you want to eat. Preferably not me or the other employees, if that's not asking too much. But move the way you move, look the way you look. There is nothing wrong with that."

Anatema's silver mask was immobile. The muscles of her face, if she had them, seemed frozen in the same neutral expression, and her third eyelid opened and closed, opened and closed, like a reptile.

"You have seen me," echoed Anatema. "You are correct. *Seen*."

They sipped their teas in silence. The dried flower of a purple poppy bloomed in contact with hot milk. Dália warmed her cold hands on the cup, blowing the vapor away and wishing she could stay there just a little longer. She would not have minded dying. If she lived, she would like to see a starry night like this one again, eating a banquet after hours of locking and unlocking the treasury's drawers.

"Should I come again tomorrow, madam?" she asked when Anatema followed her to the elevator.

YES, WITHOUT FAIL

Dália smiled and closed the wrought-iron gates. Two brown tarantulas snuck into the elevator, and she took them from the floor like they were kittens. She caressed their hairy thoraxes as she walked down the darkened corridor of the second story and left them in a safe corner. If they escaped through the window, they could avoid being eaten, but if they decided to stay, someone might adopt them as pets.

That night, she dreamed again of the attic.

She ran, stumbling, fumbling, trying desperately to find her way out of the maze of folding screens, mistaking the lacquered peacocks, the herons, the chrysanthemums. She ran without knowing why. She went around in circles in that immense and kaleidoscopic chamber, under the moonlight that invaded the stained glass of the walls.

She only stopped when her shoe got stuck in a spiderweb. The abrupt obstacle threw her onto the floor, where she fell on her knees and hands. The delicate shoe she was wearing remained in the web, while Dália found herself in the middle of a comfortable nest of colorful pillows. She groped for her foot, covered only by thin stockings, as she sat on one of the cushions.

A scarlet blindfold waited for her on one of the pillows.

She knew why it was there. It awaited her; she was meant to wear it. She blindfolded herself and lay down in the middle of the maze.

A voice called out her name, as distant as the winds battering the windows. *Dália, Dália.* She could not see anything, but she knew something moved closer to her, not for its footsteps, which were nonexistent, but for its chilly presence. It was like a hovering flame; she could sense it.

The blindfold thinned.

The presence loomed large, and she could see it now, dimmed like a shadow game. One, two, three, eight limbs. Dália understood, then, what was happening: she was not in a labyrinth, but in the centerpiece of a spiderweb.

A hand lifted her chin. Dália sighed, and the finger ran across her jaw, the curvature of her ear, the side muscle of her neck. It dropped the first strap of her dress, then the second. It forced her lips open, it pressed against her tongue, it found the warmth of her throat.

The presence consumed her, pinning her against the silk, but Dália didn't fight her. No, she searched for more contact, she pulled her closer by the hem of her robes, she ran her hand through her long hair. *Dália, Dália.*

Curious, she tried to lift the blindfold a little bit. If she did it slowly, if she was fast, if she was bold . . .

The dream was forgotten as soon as Dália woke up.

"We didn't have time to talk about your trip," commented Lionel during lunch. They were eating together in the music room, away from the other employees, since the place had the advantage of having a continuously playing gramophone that would grant them privacy. "Did you contact Cecília's father?"

"I did, but it was of no use." Dália broke one of the legs of a crispy tarantula fritter and dipped it in cocktail sauce. "He didn't care about her in the slightest."

"I didn't tell you before because I didn't want to ruin your hopes, but I already imagined that was the case." Lionel exhaled with resignation. Minerva, his cobalt-blue tarantula, ate a smaller spider at the corner of the table. "He was the one I called to convey Cecília's death."

"I never realized until now that you're the one who does that."

Lionel shook his head.

"It's not an easy task. I suppose I'm too softhearted, which is not a useful quality in my job. But I can't accept seeing bride after bride, and have them all meet the same end."

Dália touched his hand. Her fingers entwined Lionel's, feeling his hot skin and knotty phalanges. She just wanted to offer some support, and he smiled, grateful, rubbing the back of Dália's hand.

Should she say something? That she sympathized or understood? There was no time for a response, as the phone rang and the majordomo had to go upstairs to solve a problem with the power cords on the second floor. He excused himself and took a few seconds too long to break the physical contact.

Alone again, Dália went outside, toward the poppy field.

The green capsules of the flowers were marked by cuts and fat droplets of milky latex, and the petals whirled with the breeze. Dália went to the doghouse, petting the spotted head of a dalmatian.

"Do you want me to unlock the dogs?" asked Branca, who washed the dog bowls nearby. "The girls from the kitchen like to play with them, too."

Dália nodded. Branca crouched to open the panel of the kennel, and the top of her head looked pink under the sun.

"They're so sweet."

"With our folk, yes, they are. But with other animals . . ." Branca smirked. "You should see how sweet they are when they hunt."

Dália rubbed the dog's ears. They shed as she petted them, leaving black and white fur on her palm. She checked the flask in her pocket, but the result was the same as all the other previous attempts: nothing.

"How's their sense of smell?" asked Dália.

"Excellent," answered Branca. The light blue ribbon was tied around her wrist. "They can smell a rabbit from miles away."

Dália took one of the lashes and placed it near the dark snout of the animal. The dalmatian sniffed several times and curled its mouth, snarling.

"Hey, hey!" Branca held him by the collar. "What's that, animal fur?"

Dália's mouth turned into a perfect O.

"Animal?"

Before Branca could answer, Dália stood up, lifting the flask toward the sunlight. Against the natural light, she could see the "lashes" were not black, but had blue highlights, cobalt-like.

There was only one spider in the house with that coat, but she wouldn't tell anyone about her discovery, not yet.

8

Dália refused to believe in it. The more she looked at the contents of the flask, the more she noticed the bluish hue of the hair. *Minerva has been so fastidious lately,* Lionel had told her in the past week. *She always was, but in the last months, she follows me everywhere.* . . .

Everything made sense now: the sadness in his voice when he spoke of the brides, the mysterious letters addressed to Cecília, the fact that the thief only stole the doll and the envelope. When they had lunch in the music room, there was a weight in his voice that should not have been there.

Dália had spent so many years imagining, *desiring* the focus of his eyes on herself that she was surprised to see that, maybe, the problem had never been her—maybe Lionel had been in love with Cecília all along.

If he was the secret admirer, he would have hated to know that the ghost of the woman he loved roamed a locked box, day after day. That was why he also stole the fake letter, the proof of the faint connection they shared during her short life.

Dália bit the inside of her lip.

How could she tell Anatema something like this? If she

did, she would devour Lionel. Dália didn't want that to happen to him, and it wasn't fair for him to be punished for caring for Cecília. Still, Matilde died because of him, and Dália herself could have been the next victim. . . .

Anatema was the one who killed her, she had to remind herself. *Anatema is the one who killed them all.*

During dinner, she offered Anatema the usual pleasantries: polite smiles, shallow questions, comments about the food. Anatema did not seem aware of her uneasiness, telling her the details of the construction of the Capricious House, babbling about the time Torroella i Fajó brought a team of artists from several different countries to furnish the house with sculptures, paintings, and other luxurious furniture.

Even though Dália wanted to solve the mystery, she couldn't imagine herself telling the truth. Whenever she looked at Anatema, she thought only of her gaping blue mouth, ready to eat whichever employee she saw fit.

You might not believe me, but I am not the worst of my kind, said Anatema as she drank another goblet of laudanum. *Compared to some of them, I could even be described as charming, I'd say.*

Dália kept asking about other Archaic Ones to distract herself. *One of my brothers is truly terrible,* answered Anatema while the maids brought tea. *From a distance, you might think he is a regular man, but under the clothes, he is just a putrid cluster of snakes, tied to one another by the tails like a rat king. Well, he* was*; he no longer exists.*

After a week had passed since her discovery, Dália decided she had to do something about it. She knew Lionel used to work until two in the morning, and that most of his service was done on the second floor, inside the majordomo's office.

"Sleep well, Madam Anatema," said Dália when the owner of the house took her to the elevator as usual. The walls of the treasury were adorned by extravagant wisteria arrangements, dripping from their pots in blue tendrils. "Should I come tomorrow as well?"

Anatema came closer, her enormous shadow covering Dália's entire frame. Her silver face had been stuck in a constant smile these last few days, which she found both captivating and oppressive.

"As far as I'm concerned," started Anatema, her pointy finger running across the visible extension of Dália's neck. "You would never leave this place again."

Dália smiled back.

"I, on the other hand, still hope you will visit the rest of the house with me, one of these days."

Anatema bristled, the minuscule scales that coated her body rising.

MY POOR LITTLE FOOL

"There is no reason for me to go downstairs," said Anatema, her fangs sprouting from the folds of her mouth as she spoke. "What for? To collect even more disgusted, horrified sounds at the sight of my appearance? What a waste of time. I have no interest in any other little person . . ."

ONLY MISS DÁLIA

THE ONLY ONE TO EVER SEE ME

WITHOUT FLEEING LIKE A COWERING

CAT

Dália smiled one last time. She glanced at the words on the floor that urged her to be bolder, bolder.

"I pray you will change your mind, one day," she said, then flipped the lever.

Anatema disappeared slowly while the mechanical construction took her back to the second floor. It was a quarter to one, and most of the employees were already fast asleep, the lamps of the corridor dimmed to a glimmering half-light. Dália walked past the closed door of Lionel's office, where she could hear the muffled melody played by his gramophone.

Taking a deep breath, she went first to her own room, clinking the keys and pretending to open and close the lock, then she held the bunch to her chest to keep it from making sounds. Quietly, she reached Lionel's bedroom in the men's wing and knocked on the light wood, just to be sure.

No one answered.

Dália chose the residential master key and unlocked the empty bedroom. Everything happened very fast. She left the bunch of keys on the bed and opened every drawer as swiftly as she could manage. She checked behind Minerva's empty tank, inside the embedded bathroom, the wardrobe, and even in the crevices of the walls. The last place she inspected was under the mattress, where she finally found what she was looking for—a letter.

Dália held the envelope, tracing the broken seal.

The letter had no recipient nor sender, but inside was a typewritten note:

```
            DEAR CECÍLIA,
    HERE IS MY SMALL CONTRIBUTION;
   THE PROOF THAT I NEVER FORGOT YOU.
REMEMBER THAT YOU ARE LOVED, YOU ALWAYS
           WERE, ALWAYS WILL BE.
      WITH LOVE, UNTIL MY DYING DAY,
                    .
```

Dália almost dropped the letter, realizing she was shaking. She thought of putting everything back in place and pretending not to know, but her limbs acted by themselves, grabbing the keys, the envelope, and retracing the path toward the office right beside the elevator, with a bronze plaque that said: MAJORDOMO.

"Dália?" Lionel abandoned his cup of poppy tea as the soothing jazz music kept playing in the background. "Do you need anything?"

His eyes went down to her hands, one holding the bunch of keys, the other holding the envelope. Minerva walked from his arm to his shoulder, like she, too, expected a reaction from Dália.

"It seems you have discovered the truth." Lionel removed the spider carefully from his body, leaving her next to the saucer, but she returned to his arm like the stubborn creature she was. "Well then."

He stood up and retrieved the envelope, looking at the note with such a miserable expression that Dália felt like running away to pretend nothing ever happened. Instead, she stood still, waiting for an explanation that justified Matilde's death.

It wasn't right. None of the employees should have been daring enough to want one of the brides, and none of them should have betrayed Anatema. To think, of all of the people who had lived and died inside the Capricious House, Lionel would be the one to do such a thing . . .

The envelope almost slipped from his fingertips, and he held it close to his chest, crumpling the paper. Minerva touched his neck with her front legs, trying to climb the collar of his shirt.

The majordomo removed her one more time, then faced Dália.

"Dália . . ." Hair covered his face, hair the same color as

the carpet, the table, the chair. "I thought that, when you found the clues, you would understand. . . ."

"It's madness, madness," mumbled Dália. "What if Anatema knew? Betrayed under her own roof . . . How could you ignore that an affair would kill Cecília?"

The question took Lionel from his melancholy, and he blinked at Dália, puzzled. Even Minerva seemed paralyzed, back on the table, brilliant and blue even so late in the night.

"Affair? It seems you have misunderstood the direction of my affections." Lionel took Dália's hands, taking them to his lips. "I wasn't the one sending money to Cecília."

"But the letter said . . ."

"I think you must know who I mean. Who, of all the people we know, was most affected by the last bride's arrival? Who posted letters every month, who . . . ?"

Dália realized her breathing was erratic, her chest going up and down under the white shirt. *I must be getting old*, Matilde had said when Cecília first visited the house. At the time, the doctor told her to rest, and Dália went to the bedroom with her, placing several throw pillows under the keeper of the keys. Dália had even joked: *Now it just looks like you want me to succeed you sooner. . . .*

"But why? Why Matilde?"

"Because she wanted to provide for her granddaughter, of course," answered Lionel. *It's just like having a little granddaughter.* The words felt ominous now. "Only Susana and I knew. Before, she only sent money to her daughter, but after Cecília was born . . ."

"Susana?"

"I needed help to steal the second piece." Lionel touched Dália's shoulder while she kept looking at the floor. "If we hadn't done it, you would have died. Do you understand what I mean, now?"

"I thought . . ."

Lionel smiled. "You thought wrong."

"What am I supposed to do with all this information?" Dália remembered the mouth, the teeth, the pincers, the chelicerae. "If I lie to Madam Anatema . . . But if I tell her the truth . . ."

"Only one person here should do something about it, and that person is not you," replied Lionel. His droopy eyes were stained by dark circles, and his face seemed thinner in the dim light. "I made my choice."

"*Choice?*" The question came out in a strangled voice. "You won't tell. You can't . . ."

He cupped her cheek with a gentle hand, different from the beastly claws of Anatema around her neck. Lionel attempted another smile, but even like that he looked sad.

"It's the right thing to do. I had hopes she would eventually forget, but since that did not happen, and now that you're in danger again after being showered with so much attention . . ." One of his pale fingers brushed a curl that fell stubbornly on her eyes. "I told you earlier that you were mistaken regarding the direction of my affection."

Lionel bent down to kiss her, just like in one of her dreams. That was what she wanted all along, wasn't it?

For a long moment, when she parted her lips to allow him to guide her, Dália wanted to believe it was. In her reveries, she had imagined the moment where Lionel would abandon his deadpan expression and replace it with passion, right before a kiss.

Seen, yes, she was seen. Each touch reanimated her, like she was one of Anatema's courted brides, like she was made real by another person's touch, like she, somehow, was no longer just a cog in the machine of the house. Dália felt like she was floating, watching as the black jacket fell around her shoes, remembering she had a neck that could be kissed, hands that could move, a waist that could be held.

I would not have ever done this, confessed Lionel, between sighs, *if I wasn't about to die.*

The world stopped there.

Dália extinguished like a bedside lamp whose light darkens slowly. She was no longer the one who was seen, but the observer, as she had always been, Dália, just Dália. Mechanically, she asked him why, and Lionel offered a restrained smile. *It wouldn't be appropriate, considering our jobs; we have to make many sacrifices in this life.*

Dália wondered if her desires were wrong. *No,* said another part of her. It was nice, like eating battered tarantulas every day was nice, like slipping inside a warm bed at night after working all day was nice, like . . .

No, that's not how it's supposed to be, the same voice whispered. Sometimes, there were feasts instead of meals, there was fear, adrenaline, joy. Sometimes everything was real. Sometimes, she had dreams where she was tied to a spiderweb, lost in a maze, blindfolded, unable to see, but seen at last.

The only one to ever see me. The memory of the sepulchral voice was enough to make her shiver. When they were done, the two of them reclothed in their uniforms, Lionel said:

"I will ask for an audience with Madam Anatema, and I will confess everything. Face to face. So . . ." He made a small pause. "I think this is farewell."

"I can go with you," said Dália without thinking. "I can make her understand . . ."

Lionel shook his head. "There is no way of bargaining

with Anatema. I already fulfilled my last wish, which was kissing you. I don't want you to be in danger."

That didn't change Dália's mind; she knew what she had to do, and she would do it, somehow. She made Lionel promise to go with her, and she returned to her bedroom for a warm bath. She took a nap, and when she woke up, she put on the dress.

Dália searched for the mirror. It was strange to see herself in the kind of clothes usually worn by the brides. The cream-colored dress flowed down her body, and it seemed to have been tailored to flatter her complexion and follow her measurements. Every inch of it had been bought for Dália, and Dália alone.

If someone found her smiling, straightening the dress, they would call her mad. Dália, the fool who believed she could calm the monster. If she did not end up in her stomach, the next time Anatema told her to stay upstairs forever, Dália could, perhaps, say yes.

"If I don't come back," she told Una and Matilde's tarantula. "I'm sure someone will take good care of you two."

Calm and composed, Dália walked to the end of the corridor, where Lionel awaited her.

9

The mechanical click announced their arrival. Dália walked out of the elevator, opening the gates and stepping aside. Lionel followed her in silence. Despite having lived all his forty years of life in the house, the majordomo was stiff and shuddering, looking at the third floor with visible disquiet.

Come, said Dália in a small voice.

They crossed the inscription warning brides to

BE BOLD, BE BOLD

and walked to the library, where Anatema had agreed to meet Lionel.

BE BOLD, BUT NOT TOO BOLD,

the house reminded her, but the man by her side seemed incapable of seeing anything around them but his own nervousness.

Lionel knocked on the door, and Anatema's horrible disembodied voice almost pushed them down.

COME IN

Dália offered Anatema a coy smile. The Archaic One waited on the other side of the desk in her usual mantid position. The robe allowed space for her long neck covered in blue and silver scales, and her eyes were narrowed into two tight slits.

"Madam," said Dália. "This is Lionel, your majordomo."

Anatema's nictitating membrane closed and opened. Her neck extended toward them and stopped in front of Dália.

I KNEW YOU WOULD

LOOK RESPLENDENT

WEARING THIS DRESS

After she spoke, her head returned to the previous place, and Anatema looked slightly more human again.

"I hope you have an excellent reason to request this audience, majordomo Lionel," said Anatema, dropping the tearing voice. "I feel somewhat repulsed by you little men. It's a whim, yes, but as you know, I can be rather eccentric."

"Yes, ma'am, I have a good reason." Lionel bowed his head. "I'm afraid I know who stole from your treasury."

The answer got her interest.

"Who? Tell me now and I will solve the issue right away."

All traces of expression vanished from his face, and Lionel smoothed his traits into an apathetic mask.

"Matilde, the former keeper of the keys, stole the doll of your bride Cecília," replied Lionel. "Matilde was Cecília's maternal grandmother, and she spent the last twenty years sending her letters."

Dália was surprised to see how placid Anatema was. She listened to everything in silence, nodding at times.

"Well," she finally said. "That will be easy to solve. Have you searched her belongings?"

"No, ma'am, the doll was buried along with what was left of her."

"Then unearth her and bring me back my memory."

Anatema's voice was impassive, like they were speaking of a financial issue. "Good. I like simple solutions."

Lionel cleared his throat. The little color left in his complexion was gone, replaced by a chalk-white pallor.

"I have no intention of telling you where the doll is, ma'am. I only wanted you to know she was the one who did it, and there is no one else to blame for the second theft than me."

For a moment, Dália thought Anatema had stopped breathing. A shiver ran down her neck to the end of her spine, and Dália walked step by step toward the table, disturbed by the sight of Anatema's black and gray hair undulating and her silver scales bristling.

"Madam," called Dália, but she could no longer listen. "Madam, please . . ."

The floor began to tremble.

An abyssal roar came from the depths of the earth, under the Capricious House, rocking the beams and rippling the carpet, turning the wooden boards of the floor into a violent sea. Dália grabbed Lionel by the arm, dragging him toward the door.

"Run!" she yelled, but her voice was swallowed by the metallic and inhuman sound consuming the entire library.

HOW DARE YOU

STEAL

MY MEMORIES?

Anatema grew larger and larger, inflating her limbs and augmenting her body until it reached the ceiling. Before, she might have been an immense spider, greater than any human, but now she was colossal, barely fitting the limits of her own house.

Dália would have remained there, frozen and gawking at the apparition, but Lionel pulled her by the hand, running toward the spiral stairway. *RUN,* he yelled, even as the stained glass windows shattered into hundreds of sharp shards that flew everywhere, pinning the longer part of her dress to the floor. Dália didn't want to leave, she wanted to go back to the library and explain to Anatema that no, everything made sense, if only she would listen. . . .

One glance back was enough for her to know it would be impossible. Anatema grabbed one of the cauldrons of laudanum the cooks left for her and drank it all in one crass gulp, the reddish liquid running down her exposed gullet. When she finished, she threw the iron vessel to the side, breaking one of the tables in half.

Anatema darted after them, climbing the ceiling, walls, and beams, then back to the floor, all in a fast hurricane of colors and legs that destroyed everything in their wake. Like that, Dália could see that her body was indeed divided in two: a very narrow humanoid cephalothorax—with small protuberances that mimicked breasts, had they been carved in stone and smoothed out—and a fully arachnoid abdomen in shades of blue.

The dark robe billowed around her, mixing with the tangled hair, the widened neck, the claws tearing apart everything that came in their way. Lionel and Dália ran down the stairs, skipping steps until they reached the lower floor, panting.

The booming sound stopped.

Employees crowded the corridor of the second floor, exchanging concerned glances. *What was that?* they whispered, huddling together. *Is Madam Anatema . . . ?*

Dália looked up; Anatema appeared to have given up.

"She won't come down," whispered Lionel, hand clutching his own chest. "She never . . ."

The silence lasted briefly. Another screech resounded in every room, the howl of a wounded reptile, and the lengthy

Persian rug serpentined, throwing some employees against the walls. The panicked voices of the maids and electricians were smothered by the terrifying bellow coming from above, and Lionel hurried to evacuate everyone, screaming commands.

HOW DARE YOU?

echoed throughout the house. A blast of wind threw them back, and Dália grasped the cream-colored fabric of the dress as she rolled down the floor, spirals of dark hair escaping from her bun to cover her face. **HOW**, Anatema asked again, her voice thundering in each and every bone of her body.

HOW,

HOW,

HOW???

"Dália!" Lionel pulled her back to her feet. "Come!"

"I can't. Anatema . . ."

There was no time to flee. The hardened muscles of Anatema's articulated arms appeared in the stairway, then her massive body came into view, descending the exterior of the elevator's machinery, pushing a cluster of wires aside. Anatema hopped to the rug and walked above Filipa, who had failed to hide in her bedroom, but was quick enough to avoid the monstrous legs. The creature slammed a food cart to the side, spreading pies and candies all over the floor.

Before they could even consider an escape, an enlarged hand pressed Dália against the wallpaper, and the other locked Lionel from his neck to his knee.

"If you try to run again," started Anatema, the skin ungluing to reveal the hidden turquoise mouth. Lionel stared at a distant point in the ceiling to avoid the fangs and chelicerae. "I will eat all of you. But if you tell me where my treasures are . . ."

"I made my stance very clear," snapped Lionel. "I will never regret helping a friend."

Anatema turned around to look at Dália. She was still speaking to the majordomo, but her ink-blue eyes only saw her.

"So be it, then," she said, then dragged both of them back to the third floor.

Dália glanced at the ticking cuckoo clock. Hours had passed since Anatema tied her to a chair with her silk, and there was no way out other than to wait for her fate.

Lionel had been taken to another room, but Anatema decided she would stay with her in the library, just like on their very first day. Initially, Dália thought that meant she would be punished before him, and her eyes burned when she realized she would die with the owner of the house believing her a traitor, like everybody else.

It was only when Anatema crouched to her side that she understood what was going to happen next.

"I can't devour you before I finish your memory," said Anatema, spinning web for a little doll. "Where would you like to be? Your bedroom? Do you have a favorite place?"

Dália closed her eyes. She had been happy with Matilde, when she slept on a small mattress by the side of her bed, but that memory was too old. She liked to take walks in the field of poppies, hearing the dalmatians barking from far away; she liked to read; she liked to go to the kitchen when it was filled with the sweet smell of cake; she liked her deep-fried spiders . . .

Recently, she had grown fond of the folding screens of the attic maze, just like she enjoyed waiting for the moment a pale hand would offer her a plate of Turkish delight.

"The attic, or somewhere on the third floor," she answered, her voice hoarse after all the screaming from the early hours of the day. "But I don't want to be alone. I would like you to be with me, madam."

Anatema stopped weaving.

M E ?

Dália nodded. Her arms were sore after so many hours in the same position, and she leaned her cheek against a dusty shelf, offering a brief smile.

"I truly loved our dinners, madam. For a long time . . ." Her throat failed, and she had to take a deep breath to start again. "For a long time, I thought I did not exist. That working as the keeper of the keys meant that I was no more than the furniture of your house. Nobody asked me what I wanted or felt."

Anatema didn't answer. She still occupied a great deal of the library, and eight blue eyes had popped open above her mouth.

"That's my happiest memory," finished Dália.

W
I
T
H

M
E
E
e
e
.
.
.
?

Her voice decreased and her body deflated like a balloon releasing air little by little. Her appendages shrunk back to their usual size, her tagmata rearranged themselves, the robe floated around her torso and tied itself around her waist. Even her gaping mouth sewed itself around her neck, hiding pincers and returning to a state that was longer than any person, but could even look normal behind a folding screen.

Anatema stared at the miniature in progress. One of her back legs cut the web that held Dália to the chair, and the keeper of the keys pushed aside the remaining web.

Still gigantic, Anatema looked small only compared to her monstrous other form. Crouching as she weaved, she was no longer threatening, and her hair covered most of her face. An arm moved toward the candy jar and took a handful of Turkish delight. Dália went to her side and leaned her face against Anatema's hard back.

The Turkish delight prompted a pleased sound out of her throat, and Dália smiled.

"It looks beautiful."

10

The owner of the Capricious House disappeared after releasing her prisoners. She did not call the majordomo; she did not send typewritten notes. She did not ask the kitchen for food, she did not request the service of the maids, and no noise betrayed her presence. For two entire days, the employees exchanged whispers, wondering if she might have been dead.

Nobody knew the truth, but Dália knew she had to wait. Every morning was the same: she woke up, took a bath, ate her meals, and did her regular work, locking and unlocking whatever the other workers needed her to unlock. She did not mention Anatema's name at any point. When Lionel tried to talk to her, she just shook her head with a sphinxlike smile.

"I'm sure she will call us when the time is right."

A full week passed with this same routine. It was on the seventh day, during lunch, that they heard the high-pitched scream of a maid who was startled by the huge creature that came out of the carved fireplace. Anatema shook her hair, removing a cloud of dust, and went to the kitchen.

Everyone stopped what they were doing, observing her in constrained silence.

"Good afternoon," she finally said with her hissing voice, the chelicerae appearing slightly from the corners of her macabre grin. She dusted her indigo robe, ignoring the widened eyes of the people surrounding her.

"Madam Anatema." Lionel stood up at once, greeting her with a pronounced bow. Anatema looked amused by the sight of the majordomo's body twisted on himself. "Can we help you?"

"Well, yes, of course. I'm starving. Also . . ." Anatema paused, one of her arms extending to grab a live tarantula from the ceiling. She ate her in a single bite. "It seems I lost my temper the other day. The upper floor is a disaster, most of the furniture is broken and in need of repairs."

Lionel made a swift gesture for a group of women who had already eaten, and the maids hurried out of the kitchen.

"We will fix everything as quickly as possible, ma'am. We are grateful for your infinite patience."

Anatema's grin only grew. Dália looked at her, as curious as the owner of the house seemed to be, and waved her hand so she would notice her.

"Are you apologizing, madam?"

The silver scales bristled. "I already said it."

Dália repressed a giggle.

"I also came here to meet my loyal employees. There. I saw them. They saw me. That is all." She turned around abruptly. "Keeper of the keys. Follow me."

Dália grabbed the heavy bunch of keys and trailed after her, walking past rows of curious looks. The red key of Cecília's drawer felt warm against her hand.

The two went in silence to the spiral stairway, and Dália pressed the button of the elevator.

"There is something you must know." Anatema took all

the blue poppies from a vase, snapping their long stems. She placed one in Dália's hair, and the others fell on the employee's arms, spilling from between her fingers and pooling around her feet. "I no longer need a keeper of the keys. You are dismissed."

Dália blinked, paralyzed. The flowers kept cascading over her.

"Are you kicking me out of the house?"

WHO SAID SUCH A THING?

Dália could barely hold the continuous stream of poppies that kept showering over her, their blue petals covering most of the lampblack gleam of her leather shoes. Still, Anatema continued, picking flowers from other vases and letting them fall above her head.

"Madam," she interrupted, closing her eyes as petals fell over her chest. "That's too much."

Anatema stopped all of a sudden, looking stung.

"I thought you liked them. You are always looking at the flowers. In any case, why would I expel you? You really are a little fool."

The elevator arrived at the ground floor, and the front gates snapped open like a hungry mouth. Anatema climbed around its outside, as she had a week before, and opened the secondary door for Dália. When she failed to move, Anatema let out a guttural, annoyed sound.

"I told you I no longer want a *keeper of the keys*." One of her thin hands held Dália by the nape of her neck, forcing her to walk as three strong fingers buried into her skin. "Enter at once, or you will spoil the surprise."

Dália obeyed, leaving behind a procession of blue poppies and delicate leaves. The elevator ascended slowly until they reached the third floor, and the door opened with a heavy thud. One of the maids swept shards of stained glass near the treasury, while another pinned back the fallen paintings.

Anatema was already there. This time, she did not straighten her back nor did she force the mantid position she used to interact with humans, but kept climbing the walls, expecting Dália to follow. The keeper of the keys stepped on the inscription that said

LEST THAT YOUR HEART'S BLOOD SHOULD RUN COLD

and reached the attic.

At the center of the labyrinth of folding screens, a dollhouse waited for them, big enough to reach the middle of Dália's chest. Anatema took a golden key from her indigo robes and unlocked the facade to reveal the interior.

The dollhouse was a perfect replica of the Capricious House, with doll employees moving about. The cooks baked bread in the kitchens, the caretaker fed the dalmatians, Susana waited inside the elevator with a food cart, Lionel sealed letters in his office with Minerva on his shoulder, Filipa smoked opium lying on her bed, Branca held a bucket full of poppy latex.

And, above all, in the attic, a great blue spider covered Dália with flowers.

"I do not want a keeper of the keys," Anatema said again. "I want a bride."

Dália knelt in front of the house, in awe. The tips of her fingers brushed against the colorful construction, almost lifelike except for the empty faces of the tiny dolls.

"I can't accept it. It's just not possible."

Anatema withered to half her size.

I THOUGHT YOU WERE THE ONLY ONE

I THOUGHT YOU HAD SEEN ME

Dália took the golden key from her hand and added it to the bunch hooked to the loops of her pants.

"There are two issues here, Madam Anatema. First, I would like to keep guarding your keys...." Dália stood up and walked toward Anatema. She had to stand on her tiptoes to reach her face, and still she was much smaller than her. "But, more than that, I don't want to be a bride."

YOU DO NOT?

Dália pulled her down and kissed her icy skin, the texture of the scales different from anything she had ever felt before. Different, not worse. Her kisses continued down the lines of her mouth, feeling the volume of the fangs hidden underneath, her undulating neck, her marked collarbone. She laid her face on her chest, then looked up.

"I don't want to be a bride for a few days," she repeated. "I want to be a wife."

The bunch of keys fell on the floor, clinking, and the house trembled again. Anatema stretched to call the kitchen; they needed a feast as soon as possible; everyone needed to be present; then, they would celebrate. *But not now,* said Dália, taking the phone away from her. *Now, you're all mine.*

Acknowledgments

There are two different teams I would like to thank, in two different countries:

For the English translation, my agent, Lee O'Brien, and my editor, Sanaa Ali-Virani, who are both a pleasure to work with *and* extremely patient with my messy prepositions (sorry about that); Andrew Davis, who designed this lovely cover; and everyone at Tor, who turned this little fairy tale into a beautiful book.

For the original Portuguese edition, Dante Luiz, who knows why, always; Dame Blanche's editor-in-chief, Anna Martino, and copy editor, Sol Coelho, who were always encouraging and helpful; Juliana Pinho for agreeing to create the most charming illustration for the cover; and the incredible warmth Brazilian readers showed this story in spite of common complaints of arachnophobia.

About the Author

HACHE PUEYO is an Argentine-Brazilian writer and translator. She won an Otherwise Fellowship for her work with gender in speculative fiction, and her work has appeared as H. Pueyo in *The Magazine of Fantasy & Science Fiction, Clarkesworld, Strange Horizons,* and *The Year's Best Dark Fantasy & Horror,* among others. You can find her online on hachepueyo.com or on social media @hachepueyo.